*A mamma e babbo, per avermi fatto vedere
il fantastico che si nasconde nell'ordinario.*

Grazie.

TIJARAN TALES: WHITE CHILD

F. T. Barbini

Bright Pen

A Bright Pen Book

Text Copyright © F. T. Barbini 2011

Cover design by F. T. Barbini ©

British Library Cataloguing Publication Data.
A catalogue record for this book is available from the British Library

ISBN 978-07552-1349-8

Authors OnLine Ltd
19 The Cinques
Gamlingay, Sandy
Bedfordshire SG19 3NU
England

This book is also available in e-book format, details of which are available at www.authorsonline.co.uk

ACKNOWLEDGMENTS

To Robert S. Malan, my editor, for his incredible support throughout this journey, And to Sharon Bekker, for the keen eyes and the great patience.

CONTENTS

THE TRUTH BEHIND FLYING SOCKS

'Julius McCoy, get your brother off the ceiling!'

Mrs McCoy, despite her kindly nature, was not a woman to be trifled with and, seeing as she was pointing a ladle at him, Julius thought it might be wise to do as she said.

'Down. Now,' she ordered.

Julius had been focussing intently on his younger brother, who was floating happily just beneath the ceiling, but now he relaxed his mental grip. Mrs McCoy stepped underneath Michael, who plummeted into her outstretched arms, giggling delightedly.

'There is little to laugh about, young man,' she said, eyeing him severely. 'And you, Julius, now that you're 12 you should act your age. You don't want to be late for your induction, do you?' She placed Michael on the floor and, after throwing Julius an exasperated look, made her way downstairs. Julius grinned and winked at his brother, who smiled back before running off to his bedroom.

It had taken only a fraction of his mind-skills to levitate Michael up to the ceiling and guide him perfectly around the set of spotlights. Sure, the descent had been a bit too fast, but he was working on it. Besides, if he was accepted into the Zed Academy, they would teach him how to control his abilities. '*If I get in,*' he thought anxiously.

A whiff of fresh toast drifted up to his nostrils and Julius's stomach grumbled slightly, teased by the aroma. He quickly made his way out of his room, in the direction of the kitchen. The household was bustling with the usual morning activities. He could hear his mum downstairs preparing the breakfast, while Mr McCoy was doing his best to dress Michael. And that was never an easy task, given the boy's tendency for random mind-skill jokes. Julius managed to free himself from the lure of the toast long enough to pop his head into Michael's room, where their dad was trying desperately to reach a pair of socks that were floating high above the floor.

Rory McCoy was a short man in his forties, with light brown hair and dark eyes. Twelve years with his children had given him an almost permanent wrinkling of the brow. Julius used to jokingly tell him that running around after flying socks had helped to keep him in shape, but sometimes he felt genuinely sorry for him and his mother.

Normally, Julius wouldn't have interfered with Michael's routine but this morning was different, since his dad was going to fly him to the Zed Test Centre, so he decided to speed things up a little. He locked his eyes on the socks and, with a small mind-push, thrust them down into his father's hands, before silently retreating back into the corridor. However, by the time Julius reached the kitchen, Mr McCoy was once more being challenged, this time by a pair of airborne shoes.

'I would like five slices of toast,' said Julius, plonking himself down at the table, 'and three eggs please!'

'You're lucky it's such a big day, young man, or I might not have

given you even *one* slice,' said his mother setting a
front of him and ruffling his hair before turning bac

Jenny McCoy was a tall, slim woman. Her dark, w
a beautiful and elegant face where a pair of bright b
smiled kindly. Julius strongly resembled her, in that he was tall and
had similarly blue eyes and the same aquiline features. Thick dark
hair flowed down to his shoulders, except for several jagged strands
which hung loosely around his ears and forehead.

'You all set?' she asked.

He nodded, and then quietly asked her, 'Do you think the
Academy will take me?'

'You tell me if they don't,' she said, while buttering a slice of toast.
'I'm counting on a bit of peace and quiet around here.'

Julius smiled, but he sensed just a hint of sadness and tension
in her voice. Over the course of the last 12 years, Jenny and Rory
McCoy had been treated to regular displays of their son's mind-skills.
He was well aware that they had been eagerly anticipating the day he
would be old enough to take the test. In truth, they had known they
were in for a rough ride from the start; ever since their first visit to
the family Mind Doctor, Dr Flip, all those years ago. He had stared
at them from above the rim of his glasses, a mixture of excitement
and disbelief on his face.

'I have been a Mind Doctor since 2830,' he had said, waving
Julius's Brain Augmentation chart at them, 'and I have never seen
such potential in one so young. Incredible – still in diapers, but he's
pure Zed Academy material, if ever I've seen it. How many of your
ancestors fought in the Chemical War?'

The McCoys had looked at each other, speechless. The War, though
it had ended some 300 years before then, had given rise to certain

...ced mental abilities for generations afterwards. It was in no way ...nsistent – very few actually developed any mind-skills of note – so Julius's results were all the more surprising, since neither they nor their own parents had ever displayed any similar talent. However, after several weeks of intense surprises, such as Julius rocking himself in his cot while hovering a few feet off the ground, they had grown used to it, as any other parents in their position would have. Nonetheless, it had come as a bit of a relief when Dr Flips had announced that the newly born Michael possessed only a hint of his brother's mind-skills. Sure, he would be able to levitate the odd sock or two, but it was unlikely he would ever qualify for the Academy.

Still, Julius suspected the tension in his mother's voice was more due to the strange news that had been popping up lately on the Space Channels than any nerves on her son's behalf. There had been reports of frequent meetings between the Curia – the political heart of Zed – and the Earth Leader, which had caused a series of rumours about an imminent war involving Zed Academy and the Arneshians. Although the news was probably unfounded, it was a given that they would still be worried about the possibility of their son heading towards trouble.

Just then his father entered the room, closely followed by Michael, who looked awfully pleased with himself.

'I've just got up and I'm already tired,' said Mr McCoy, sounding slightly out of breath. 'I wonder why ...' he finished, flashing a disapproving look at Michael.

The boy assumed a sheepish expression and then turned quickly to his mother: 'Can I go with Julius?'

'No, Michael,' she answered. 'You have to go to school. Besides, they wouldn't let you in – you're only ten.'

Michael frowned and bent his head over his cereal bowl. He could smell defeat a mile away.

'I promise I'll tell you everything when I get back tonight,' said Julius, in an effort to cheer him up.

Michael nodded and gave him a little smile.

At that moment, the house computer came online and its metallic voice intoned: 'One female visitor approaching front door. Doorbell will ring in ten, nine, eight ...'

'I'll get it Julius. You go and get ready. If we leave early enough, we might beat the traffic,' said Mr McCoy, walking out into the hall.

Julius ran upstairs to his bedroom. He had prepared his bag a week in advance and then checked it every night since. Together with the invitation chip, he was required to bring his Brain Augmentation chart, a document provided by Dr Flip, which certified his brain development since birth. Julius sincerely hoped its contents were good enough for the staff at the test centre. He grabbed his black leather jacket from the wardrobe and swung the backpack over his shoulder. When he returned to the kitchen, a young girl was sitting at the table, drinking a glass of milk.

'*Konnichiwa*, Julius,' she said, smiling from beneath a milky moustache.

'Hey, Morgana. Got everything? Nice 'tache by the way,' said Julius, handing her a napkin from the table.

'Oops. Thanks,' she said, cleaning her lips. 'I've checked three times this morning. The last thing I need is to arrive there without my invitation chip.'

Julius had been friends with Morgana Ruthier ever since her family had moved to Edinburgh eight years ago. She was slightly taller than him, with long, straight, black hair which outlined a pair of lovely green, almond shaped eyes – compliments of her Japanese mother. By all accounts though, she had two mothers, seeing as Mrs McCoy treated her very much like the sister Julius had never had.

'All right children, it's time to go now,' said Mr McCoy, plucking his jacket from the coat stand.

Michael waved goodbye from over his cereal bowl, but kept very quiet. Mrs McCoy walked them outside in her dressing gown, imparting some last minute advice about keeping calm and being polite to their instructors. 'Just do what they ask you to do. Don't show off. And don't …'

'Yes, yes. As if!' Julius blurted out, rolling his eyes.

Morgana laughed, and while pushing Julius into the back of the fly-car, she turned to Mrs McCoy. 'I'll make sure he behaves. Don't worry.'

'Rory, call me as soon as you know,' said Jenny, retreating back into the doorway.

Mr McCoy waved to his wife and climbed into the driver's seat. Their fly-car, the Bumble Bee 5000, was his latest purchase. He had always been an original when it came to choosing his cars, and this one was no exception. It did look like a giant metal bumblebee for a start, from the stripy black and yellow lines to a pair of tiny wings on the roof – for show rather than functionality, although he always insisted that they helped with the aerodynamics. When it lifted off the road, anyone within a thirty yard radius was treated to the deep buzzing sound of its engine, as if all the men in the neighbourhood had switched on their electric razors at the exact same moment.

It was this sound that now filled the air as Mr McCoy guided the car out of their front drive, and Julius's mind wandered off, conjuring up a hundred different pictures of exactly what awaited him at the Academy.

The Zed Test Centre for the United Kingdom and Ireland was located in the outskirts of Cumbria, on a plain surrounded by hills. From Edinburgh, it was a flight of roughly forty minutes, following the Air One to Carlisle, then the Wind Four to Maryport. The Air One crossed the Southern Uplands and entered Galloway over the river Esk. It was a lovely journey in the springtime, soaring above the lush green fields dotted with the white shapes of newborn lambs below.

Although the traffic on the skyway wasn't too heavy, several other vehicles were whizzing past at different speeds and altitudes, some quite recklessly too. They, however, were floating peacefully along. The sun was shining down, unhindered by any clouds, making the car's outer shell glimmer. As an added little flourish, all Bumble Bee fly-cars had their own unique brand of paint, which smelled incredibly like honey. The heat of the mid-morning sun was intensifying that delicious smell so much that a number of seagulls had actually tried to peck at the paint before flying off in disgust.

Inside the car, the passengers had been quiet ever since leaving town. Morgana, who normally loved the countryside, was far too nervous to admire the view and was twisting and stretching a corner of her shirt with sweaty hands. When she could no longer bear the silence, she turned to Julius. 'I'm so nervous. I spoke with Kaori yesterday. She told me that I shouldn't worry because the test isn't really that difficult. But I can't help it.'

Kaori was Morgana's sister, and a third year student at Tuala, one of Zed's three schools. Of course, Morgana devoured any and all news she could pry from Kaori, and was always more than happy to excitedly pass that information on to Julius. No one was allowed within Zed's grounds except its members, but in Satras, its only civilian town, school students could receive visits from their families. As such, Morgana had been able to visit her sister twice during the mid-winter holidays, and both times she had faithfully reported back all that she had seen and done there to a decidedly envious Julius.

Today, though, he wasn't overly keen on talking about Zed. With the test looming so near, he felt it better not to jinx anything by assuming he would pass – just in case. So he nodded absently to her as she talked and kept his thoughts to himself. He was getting terribly anxious now. His stomach felt like it was on fire, while his skin was covered in goose bumps. He turned his attention to the skyway and realised they had just hopped onto the Wind Four. After a further ten minutes of whizzing along, they came across a blue signpost on the left of the skyway which read: "ZED TEST CENTRE. Reduce altitude now."

'Over there,' cried Mr McCoy, pointing to the ground excitedly.

Julius and Morgana simultaneously leapt over to the left window, causing the Bumble Bee to tilt to one side. There, below them, the Zed Test Centre came into view. As they drew closer, Julius noted how it was divided into three sectors – a landing area enclosed within long rows of shrubs, a car park next to it, and the main building. What caught his attention most, however, was the round, metallic silver building in the far sector. The lower curve of the sphere disappeared into the ground where four black iron arms emerged from the surrounding flowerbeds and hooked into it, holding the entire structure in place. What appeared to be the main entrance – a large circular doorway – yawned open above a flight of metal stairs that led up to it from a paved square, which Julius saw was bustling with movement.

The Bumble Bee slowly descended towards the runway and headed for the landing area, which was flanked by two rows of tiny yellow lights embedded in the concrete. The fly-car landed smoothly and hovered along the track towards a line of toll booths, where it stopped.

'Good morning, sir. Two for the test?' called the guard, nodding at Julius and Morgana.

'Oh, no – it's just me. They're here for moral support,' replied Mr McCoy with a grin. The guard stared back at him and raised one eyebrow quizzically.

'Dad!' Julius implored through clenched teeth. 'Not really the time.'

Mr McCoy cleared his throat and quickly handed over the invitation chips. The guard looked suspiciously at him and inserted them into his computer. A few seconds later, a holographic screen flickered to life in the space between the booth and the fly-car with pictures and personal details of the two children.

He quickly switched his gaze from the screen to the children. 'Well, I don't know about your driver here, but you two certainly appear to be in order. Enter the car park via C sector. Your space is number fourteen. Have a good day,' he said, flashing a cheeky smile at them.

Mr McCoy laughed nervously as he took the chips back and handed them over to Julius. Steering the Bumble Bee forward, he followed the road to the left and brought them to a halt at their allocated space. There, they quickly exited the car and headed along the walkway. The fly-car park was already filled with the most bizarre and colourful vehicles on the market. While Mr McCoy passed comment on the latest models – 'The Dung Beetle 1000, now that's an interesting piece of machinery, but you can bet it doesn't smell as nice as my Bee!' – Julius and Morgana were gazing at the main building, where dozens of children were making their way through its entrance.

Julius noticed that the adults weren't going in with them but were instead being directed to a small waiting room to the right. He pointed this out to his father, who was satisfied once he saw that it had windows all around so that he could continue admiring the fly-cars.

Once in the square, Mr McCoy stopped. 'I'll be waiting for you next door. You will both do well. Just stay focused.' He started towards the waiting room but after a few steps turned around and called back to his son: 'Oh, and Julius, try to leave the building standing once you're done, will you?'

Julius grinned and waved him away. Together with Morgana, he walked towards the main door and looked up. The oval emblem of Zed towered over the entrance. It showed the Moon, glowing white and full in a starry black sky. The Zed lunar perimeter was a shimmering dot in its centre. Morgana drew a deep breath and said, 'Come on Julius – let's go book our tickets for the Moon.'

THE ZED TEST

When Julius entered the building, he found himself in a large, well-lit reception area. A guard in a grey uniform was directing everybody to join a long, snake-like line to the enrolment desk. Except for a female voice shouting 'NEXT!' at regular intervals, the room was surprisingly quiet.

Julius looked around. The walls on either side of the hall were covered with portraits of people that he didn't recognise. All of them were wearing black suits with numerous medals pinned to their chests. Under each frame, was a small golden plaque bearing the name of the person portrayed. He noticed that one picture was much larger than the rest and was placed on its own high above the reception desk. Although it was quite far for him to read the inscription, he instantly knew who the man in the portrait was. In fact, there was not one person on Earth who didn't know of him: Marcus Tijara. He was the man who had almost singlehandedly brought Earth into the Space Era, researched the White and Grey Arts and most important of all in Julius's opinion, created the Zed Lunar Perimeter.

'Julius, look,' said Morgana tapping excitedly on his shoulder.

She was pointing at three full-size portraits to their left.

'This is Roland Kloister, the Grand Master of Kaori's school, Tuala. And this is Edwina Milson, the Head of Sield School. Which means that this man here is Carlos Freja, the current Grand Master of Tijara School. Kaori said that people speak of him as being the true heir of Marcus Tijara.'

Julius stared, fascinated by Freja's portrait. It was difficult to tell what his age was. His body looked tall and sturdy, his hair dark and short, but his face seemed worn and his intense grey eyes were surrounded by lines. Julius thought that, if he was accepted into Zed, he would want to go to Tijara and study under Carlos Freja. In that moment, he felt such admiration for this man who he did not even know that a sense of guilt crept over him because he realised that he had never felt like that about anyone, not even his own father. Ashamed, he pulled his eyes away from the picture.

Beside him, Morgana was looking above the heads of the other children in an effort to see how far they were from the desk.

'At least the queue is moving quickly,' she said.

'Good, 'cause I *really* need the toilet,' said a voice behind them.

Julius and Morgana turned around and then looked upward. Seated in a hovering wheelchair, a grinning boy looked down at them. Beneath a bed of tangled brown hair, two hazelnut eyes moved nervously from Julius to Morgana. After a brief awkward silence, the boy offered his hand.

'Hi. I'm Faith. From Ireland.'

Morgana, who had always been more relaxed with strangers than Julius, grabbed his hand and shook it vigorously. 'Hi. I'm Morgana, and this is Julius. From here. Well kinda – I'm actually from Japan, but my Dad is Scottish. That's why I'm doing the test here.'

The boys nodded to each other. Morgana seemed quite happy to talk away while they were waiting but Julius was still too nervous for that. So he kept quiet and occasionally dragged Morgana forward in the queue by her arm.

'That's a really flashy transport you've got there,' said Morgana, examining Faith's wheelchair from every angle. 'A Lady Bird 300, but with the electric core of an early Grass Hopper model. How unusual.'

'Wow, I'm impressed,' replied Faith. 'I haven't met many girls who would know the model of me chair, let alone noticing that the core was different. Are you into engineering?'

'She wants to be a spaceship pilot,' cut in Julius from over his shoulder.

Morgana blushed a little and smiled. 'I *would* like to.'

'That's wonderful,' said Faith. 'It's no easy job either. I wanna be a spaceship engineer and build the most amazing ships you'll ever see. Meantime, I'm practising on me chair. By using different parts, not only can I get it to spin, but also to hover and jump. I'm working on making it fly right now. I've kept the wheels functioning though, 'cause you just never know. Me friend Roy Bray back home – that would be Dublin by the way – broke down one day and his wheels were only there for show so I had to tow him all the way to his house. By the time we got there, his tires had gone and he was sending sparks everywhere like a firework,' finished Faith in a fit of laughter.

'I would have liked to have seen that,' said Morgana, giggling.

Even Julius was smiling despite his nervousness. Under the puzzled stares of several people, and because they were getting closer to the desk, they managed to pull themselves together.

Eventually, it was Julius's turn to enrol. A long faced lady stared gravely at him from behind the desk.

'Name-chip-documents,' she cried, in one breath.

'Julius McCoy,' blurted out Julius, startled.

He quickly handed her his folder. She didn't seem willing to wait for even one second.

'She's probably been doing this since dawn,' thought Julius.

The lady kept hold of his invitation chip and folder and slammed a visitor pass onto the desk. Before Julius could even say thanks, she raised her face and shouted, 'NEXT'.

Beyond the desk, a guard asked Julius to enter a room on the left. He waved back at Morgana and did so. The new space was long and bare, and had all sorts of monitors and what looked like a metallic tunnel structure on the far end. Eight boys were already sitting along the wall near the entrance. Julius moved next to a square faced boy, with rather large shoulders and an expression of contempt on his face. The visitor pass around his thick neck said that his name was Billy Somers. Julius was about to sit down when a whistling Faith entered the room and positioned himself next to him.

Somers glanced over disdainfully at Faith: 'If he's not worried about the physical test, we really shouldn't be,' he said with a snigger, to no one in particular and clearly without any concern that he might be heard.

Faith stared blankly at him for a few seconds and suddenly broke out into a broad grin. He then turned his attention to the various devices in the room as if nothing had happened. Somers, like Julius and the rest of the boys, was caught off guard for a moment by Faith's reaction, but any further retaliation was cut short by two men in white coats who entered the room and shut the door behind them. One of them was carrying a small pile of folders and walked directly towards a desk at the back of the room where he sat down; the other one stopped in front of the boys.

'Gentlemen, this is your physical test. We don't have time to waste so when I call your name step forward to the Tunnel Scan and walk – I repeat walk – through it.' He then looked at a small blonde boy. 'Taun, Roger. Follow me.'

He turned and walked towards the large device, with the little boy hurrying behind him. Julius watched Roger Taun approach the Tunnel Scan and disappear under its thick metal arch. He noticed that everybody else was watching intently, except Faith, who was examining his fingernails. The doctors worked fast. Julius watched each boy walk through the tunnel and leave the room, until his turn came. When he stepped under the Tunnel Scan one of the doctors told him to look straight ahead. The tunnel was about twenty feet long and rather dark. While he walked, he could see numerous coloured lights blinking on and off around him, accompanied by tiny beeping sounds. When he stepped outside, he saw a wide and long screen to his left that showed all the information they had gathered from his body. He didn't have time to read any of it though because his full skeleton suddenly appeared on the screen, staring back at him. The word "PASS" flashed in green across it.

'Move along now. Leave through that door,' said one of the doctors, pointing at the exit.

Julius returned to the corridor and joined the others, who were waiting for everyone to finish their medical tests. They were all quiet and he was pleased to see he wasn't the only fidgety one. He looked towards the reception, noting that it was still full of children, while dozens more were swarming through the front door. Julius briefly thought that at that very moment, across the planet and on each of the Earth colonies, all children aged 12 were being examined in their own country's Zed Test Centre. Only one hundred of them would make it to Zed though, and he strongly hoped that Morgana and he were good enough to be among the chosen ones.

The medical test had been fine and that was no small relief, but the hardest part was about to begin. They were going to test his mind-skills, on which his chances of entering Zed would rest entirely. How they would do that, however, Julius had no idea.

'I hope they ask me to start a fire or move something with my mind,' he thought, but that immediately made him recall that he still wasn't very good at putting the fires out afterwards, and that Michael's landing that very morning had not gone too smoothly. For the next few minutes, Julius mentally went through all the skills he'd ever used and concentrated on the correct dose of energy to use for each of them. Like his father had said, he really didn't want to destroy anything, which *had* been known to happen.

When Faith finally joined them, a different man in a grey uniform walked towards them.

'Follow me gentlemen. Single file and do not lag behind,' he said.

He then turned and started down a staircase. They hurried after him, Julius accompanied by the gentle hum of Faith's chair behind him. A few minutes later they reached a small room. It was unfurnished, except for several bulky cardboard boxes spread to one side of the room. Some of them were flattened and piled against one of the walls. A gangly man with dark hair starkly flattened against his head grabbed a handful of small black objects from an open box and stamped them indelicately to each of the boys' foreheads.

'Thethe are thelf-adhethive micro-chipth,' he said in a bored voice.

Everyone looked at each other puzzled, while someone grunted in the back. Even the guard was straining to suppress a laugh. The man, clearly oblivious of the reaction to his lisp, took no notice and continued with his chant: 'Do not remove them until you are told to do tho. Your brain activity will be tranthmitted through them and recorded on thenthor boxeth during your tetht. There are five luminouth pointh on the chip. When all of them turn red, you will hear a beeping thound in your head. That ith your cue to move to the exit,' finished the man.

Once out of the room, it took the group a little while to regain their composure but, once they had recovered sufficiently, the guard led them along a narrow, descending corridor.

'We must be underground,' said Julius to Faith, who nodded nervously in agreement. It was an obvious statement to make but now that the laughter had passed he felt anxiety creeping back. Between the medical test, the chip on his forehead and walking along artificially illuminated, empty corridors, he felt as if he was on a conveyer belt.

'I can see why Kaori said that the test's not really difficult,' thought Julius, upset. He was being scanned and tagged, but nobody was interacting with him or asking him to prove himself. He was about to share his feelings with Faith when the guard huddled them all in front of a double door. He then pushed a button and a wall came down behind them, enclosing them in a small space. A few seconds later, the door in front of them opened suddenly and Julius felt a wave of energy passing through him that made his hair stand on end, while his ears were trying to adjust to the loud noises assaulting him from every direction. He was staring at the biggest room he had ever seen.

17

'Holy Fagioli! This room's gotta be at least fifty feet high,' shouted Faith.

'No kidding,' replied Julius. If Faith's estimation was anything to go by, then the room must have been easily 300 feet long. He saw dozens of sensor-boxes all along the walls; beneath them numerous adults in white coats and helmets were busy jotting down notes on their pads. In the corners, large computerised panels flashed constantly. If Julius thought that the sidelines were busy, the middle of the room was positively chaotic. Hordes of boys were running around while boxes, chairs and the occasional desk zoomed along the ceiling. Several small fires burned brightly here and there. From what he could tell, they were seemingly using their mind-skills for an obstacle course of some sort, only there was no *visible* course. Each person was acting independently, performing whatever task they chose, from shifting objects with their minds, to starting fires. Some just stared blankly at the teachers. The lights on their foreheads were showing different colours. The majority of them were yellow, some were green, and only one boy, Julius noticed, had two red lights on his forehead.

'They look like little running Christmas trees,' said Faith.

'What are they doing?' asked Julius, incredulous.

Without warning, the guard behind them blew a whistle.

'Your turn. Move it!' he shouted.

They stepped into the crowd anxiously, as if they were walking through a panic-stricken herd of buffaloes, but it took Julius only a few moments to adjust to the chaos around him.

'I suppose they just want me to show my skills,' thought Julius. At that moment, he heard a loud and clear voice inside his head: *'Make them fly!'*

He didn't recognise the voice but he instinctively knew it was a command. In front of him, he saw two little boys attempting to create a fire. Julius concentrated and fixed his gaze on them. Instantly they both levitated off the ground, puzzled expressions on their faces. When they were two feet above the floor and bouncing like yo-yos in midair, they started to scream, but among all the chaos no one heard them. Julius kept his mind locked on them and shot them across the room. When he thought that they looked green enough, he gently landed them back on the floor. He then touched his forehead, trying to figure out if his sensors had gone off, but to his frustration he couldn't tell. He sidestepped as a box flew past his head and glanced around, looking for the next challenge. Suddenly the same voice popped into his head: *'Quick, danger above you!'*

Julius looked up – a fire extinguisher was plummeting through the air towards Faith, who was busy turning someone else's small fire into a blazing furnace. Behind him, the owner of the fire extinguisher was running with his nose pointed to the ceiling trying to regain control of it, oblivious of Faith's bonfire. Julius locked his eyes onto the fire extinguisher and stopped it a couple of feet above Faith's head. At the same time, he ordered Faith to halt the boy behind him. He did this wordlessly, with his mind. Faith promptly extended his hand towards the boy, who stopped dead in his tracks as if he had hit an invisible wall. Julius then landed the extinguisher gently on Faith's lap, who took it and put out his fire. Julius let out a sigh of relief and, walking towards Faith, looked down at the ashes of the bonfire – a bright crimson flame instantly sprung from the ground, lighting up the room.

'Show off,' said Faith laughing.

At that moment, Julius felt a strong buzzing sensation in his head.

'Your sensors are all red! Am I lit up too?' shouted Faith over the noise.

'Yeah! That was quick. We've gotta get out of here,' replied Julius. 'Lead on.'

They jostled their way through the crowd, Julius moving people out of their path with small mind-pushes. Once out of the room, the buzzing in their ears stopped. There were ten cubicles lined in front of them. A man told them to queue at different ones.

'Good luck,' said Julius.

'Same to you,' answered Faith before they got separated.

When Julius finally sat down, a pretty young lady in a white coat smiled at him and, with a pair of tweezers, peeled the chip off his forehead. He was knotting his hands together, unable to sit still.

'Are you nervous?' she asked him, kindly.

Julius nodded and tried to smile, but his mouth had dried up. He watched her place the chip into a machine that looked like a microwave. She then closed the door and a red light flashed on. He sat there for what seemed like an age. Seconds felt like years. He was glad to be in a cubicle where no one could see him, for in that moment he was sure he had failed and that the lady was going to tell him that they were sorry but he just wasn't good enough. Finally, a green light blinked on and the machine printed out several pages of charts and symbols that Julius couldn't understand. He looked at the woman. She looked at the charts, wide-eyed. With an encouraging, surprised smile she looked back at Julius. 'I believe congratulations are in order.'

Julius's face broke into the biggest grin, totally at a loss for words.

'Follow the corridor,' said the lady, 'There is a waiting room two floors up and on the left. All tests should be over in a couple of hours. Someone will need to see you before you can go.'

Julius thanked her and walked past her desk into the corridor beyond. The noise slowly subsided behind him. He went up the stairs in a blissful trance and eventually found himself in front of the waiting room. As he entered the room, he was relieved to see that Morgana was already there, talking enthusiastically to a red-haired girl. When she saw him, she ran towards him, grabbed his shirt and looked into his eyes.

'Do you know what this means?' whispered Morgana excitedly. 'It means that WE-ARE-IN!'

Julius was beaming. He still couldn't believe it. His stomach was full of butterflies. He was so charged up that he felt as if he could have lifted the roof off the building with just a blink of his eye. He looked around and saw two people chatting at one of the tables and, in another corner on his own, sat a very smug-looking Billy Somers intently reading a magazine.

Julius realised that, of all the dozens of children he had seen that morning, only six were sitting in that room. He was proud to be among them and more so because Morgana was there too. He also hoped that Faith would join them soon since, without him, Julius could not have displayed his abilities so clearly or finished the test so quickly. Besides, Faith had performed well and had shown that he was surprisingly receptive to Julius's mind-messages. Before then, only Morgana had ever responded so quickly to Julius, and they had known each other for many years.

As if in answer to his wish, the waiting room door opened. With the happiest expression, Faith entered the room followed by an officer, who took a seat in the corner. Julius and Morgana went over to congratulate him. As they walked past where Somers was sitting, Julius noticed his smugness had been replaced by a mixed expression of shock and disgust. He looked as if he was about to burst, but obviously thought better of saying anything with an officer present. As Faith took his place next to Julius, he flashed a cheeky grin in the direction of the now positively furious Billy Somers.

For the next two hours everyone in the room, with the exception of Somers, chatted about the events of that morning, sharing detailed descriptions of their tasks. They all agreed on how lucky they had been to make it through.

'Anyway, what's the story with that room of chaos? People could have hurt themselves,' said the red-haired girl in a thick Welsh accent. Morgana had introduced her as Leslie Rogan.

'It's so they can test your skills under pressure of course,' answered Faith. 'They figure that when you're in trouble you don't have time to think, so they want people who are quick. Speaking of which, Julius, next time you send me a mind e-mail like you did before, do it gently. You almost blew me brain off!'

'Oh, I'm sorry. Next time I'll come and ask your permission first,' said Julius mockingly.

'Did you really speak with Faith?' asked Alan Cross, one of the other selected people. 'I mean, I could hear the messages from the teachers, but I couldn't really speak back.'

'Sure he did,' cut in Morgana. 'Julius is very good at that. When we were six, we used to team up at card games and cheat all our parents' friends out of their small change. I would challenge them, he would stand behind them, look at their cards, and then tell me what they were with his mind.'

'Remind me never to play cards with you, Julius,' said Faith, raising an eyebrow.

Finally, the door opened. A man in a navy blue uniform entered and stopped in the middle of the room, facing the group. He was tall and athletic and, although his expression was rather stern, he had a young, attractive face. He looked at each of them in turn and for a few moments not a sound could be heard. Julius grew a little uncomfortable under his gaze. As his eyes moved to the next person, Julius could have sworn that he had smiled almost imperceptibly at him.

'I am Master Cress, Second in Command of the Tijara School,' he said. His clear voice echoed in the room. 'You have been selected to join the Zed Academy. It is a great honour but also the end of life as you know it.'

With that, he reached into his pocket and drew out several small envelopes. 'Marion Lloyd and Billy Somers, step forward. You are to join the Sield School.'

He handed them an envelope each, which they took before stepping back again.

'Alan Cross and Lesley Rogan – Tuala School,' he continued.

Julius could see that Morgana was quite disappointed, because she had really wanted to join her sister, Kaori, at Tuala.

'Julius McCoy, Morgana Ruthier and Faith Shanigan – Tijara School.' They moved forward to receive their envelopes. Julius was pleased to see that he wasn't the only one who was trembling nervously – Faith's chair was practically vibrating beneath the excitement of its owner.

Julius looked at the envelope that had his name printed on it. Next to it, they had written "1MJ". Morgana had told him that all first and second year students were called Mizki Junior, and that Mizki was the name of the scientist who had first studied mind-skills alongside Marcus Tijara.

'The envelope contains a microchip with all the necessary information that you and your parents need to read,' continued Cress. 'On Sunday, the 31st of August, you are to report here at 08:00 hours. A shuttle will fly you to the Zed departure centre in Prague. Latecomers will, of course, remain here. You are now free to go,' he finished. With that he nodded to the group and left the room without so much as a second glance.

'That guy needs to chill,' exclaimed Faith, once the door had closed.

That made them all burst into laughter. All except Somers, that is, who simply walked out of the room with his nose upturned.

'And *he* could do with the same therapy,' added Julius, pointing to Somers, adding fuel to their laughter.

He could feel the tension of the morning ebbing slowly away and being replaced by a sense of relief. Julius was struck by a certainty that he would always remember this moment as one of genuine, shared happiness between a group of people who had just realised their greatest dream.

Nathan Cress stood peering through the window of his office, which overlooked the main entrance. His eyes followed Julius as he left the building. As soon as the boy had disappeared into the fly-car park, a beeping noise caught his attention. He turned towards the centre of the room and crossed his arms in front of him.

'Good day, Marcus.'

The holographic shape of the Grand Master Tijara, Marcus Freja, appeared in the middle of the room.

'And to you, Nathan,' said Freja. 'I trust you have good news.'

'You were right. The boy's mind-skills are off the charts and balanced right across the board. And he hasn't even started his training yet,' said Cress with a tinge of excitement in his voice. 'He is a natural White Child.'

Freja nodded. 'Perfect. Salgoria must not know, or she will go after him too. Her threat is growing as we speak, but we shall be ready for her when the time comes. Train him hard; keep him safe. You know what to do.'

'Of course. Leave that to me,' said Cress, as the hologram slowly faded.

THE ROAD TO THE MOON

On the morning of the 31st of August, heavy black clouds covered the sky above the Zed Test Centre. Nothing could be seen around the building but pouring water. Julius stood at the window of a waiting room, watching the rain draining away into the flowerbeds. At that moment, Morgana came running across the paved square. Before entering through the circular door, she turned and waved to her family, who were standing near their fly-car, huddled under an umbrella. Because parents were not allowed into the centre, Julius had had to say goodbye in the Bumble Bee. The McCoys had enjoyed a long and cheerful meal together the night before, during which Jenny and Rory had given Julius plenty of good advice. Mrs McCoy had shed a few tears that morning and decided to give Julius his yearly dosage of kisses and hugs, all the way from Edinburgh to Maryport. Mr McCoy had been very excited ever since the beginning of that week. He hadn't even seemed to mind that Julius, impatient for his departure, had gone a little out of control with his skills. The only time that he'd had to reprimand his son was when half of the bathtub had disappeared, while he was in it. Michael, on the other hand, seemed to have taken Julius's leaving very badly. When his brother had told him about his test back in April, Michael had been very excited, but as the months had passed, he had grown quieter and quieter. The realisation that it would be another two long years before he would have the chance to join Zed, and therefore be reunited with his brother again, had put him in a miserable mood.

'You can come and visit me in mid-winter,' Julius had told him in the fly-car. 'I'll show you Satras and the Hologram Palace, and we can play games all day.'

The idea of playing with his brother in a Hologram Palace had had a soothing effect on Michael, who had squeezed his brother tightly. 'You're the best Julius … and not just because of the Hologram Palace.'

'I love you, Mickey,' Julius had said, hugging him tighter.

Thinking of Michael made Julius smile. He had promised him that he would write as often as he could and he intended to keep to his word.

Just then, Morgana walked into the room, leaving behind a trail of water.

'I have now crossed the line between being wet and *being* water,' she said, dumping her soaking rucksack on the floor.

Julius helped her remove her coat. 'Seen anybody else in the parking lot?' he asked.

'Yes. There were five fly-cars all steamed up,' answered Morgana. 'I think there was a lot of talking and crying going on. It took me a good hour to leave home. My granny didn't want to let me go. She was so upset that in the end my Mum decided to stay behind with her.'

'I will miss your granny,' said Julius, 'especially her amazing choc-toffee-coffee pie. Who knows what they're going to feed us up there.'

'Only the best cuisine!' exclaimed Faith, entering the room and turning Morgana's trail of water into a puddle. 'It was in the chip that Cress gave us. You haven't read it, have you? Tut, tut.'

'Hi Faith, does that chair of yours float too?' asked Julius, watching water drip off it and onto the floor.

'Yes, and it's also waterproof,' he answered. 'However, I am not. Can you help me to get this coat off please? It weights a ton.'

Julius helped him while Morgana took his rucksack and put it next to hers.

'What did you guys bring in the end?' she asked. 'It took me forever to decide.'

'That's because you're a girl,' teased Julius.

'And *you* mister, are very predictable. I bet you brought music, history books and your Tolkien collection, which by the way, you must have read at least thirty times already,' answered Morgana wryly.

Each student was only allowed to bring one bag, weighing no more than five kilograms. The school would provide every essential, from toothbrush to underwear, to classroom materials. They were also told not to bring any spare clothing. It was true that Julius had packed quickly and that Morgana had been mostly right: he had packed everything that she had said and also an extra chip containing the addresses of his friends and family. His rucksack was pretty light, but he knew that whatever he might need could be found in Satras.

'What's in *your* bag then? I bet you brought pictures of airports,' said Julius, dismissing her last remark.

'Actually, I put some music and books on my chips. I also brought a copy of my favourite world landscapes and the encyclopaedia of the history of aviation,' said Morgana.

'Books and music for me too,' added Faith. 'Plus me trusty repair kit for the chair. I never leave the house without it.'

Gradually the other four students arrived. Billy Somers continued to avoid any interaction with the group, as if it would contaminate him somehow. Julius was grateful for Somers's quiet attitude – this was an exciting day for everyone, and nobody needed a spoiler.

At eight o' clock sharp, the door opened and a middle-aged woman in a grey suit entered the room. 'Attention please,' she said in a firm voice. 'Behind you are two doors leading to changing rooms – left for the ladies and right for the gentlemen. Inside you will find a bag with your name on it. I want you to change into your uniform and place your civilian clothes in the bag. Leave them there. They will be sent back to your families. You have 15 minutes.'

Julius grabbed his rucksack and followed Alan Cross into the changing room. There were four grey packs lined up in the centre of the room. Julius found his own one and dragged it to the nearest bench. Excited, he pulled out a pair of combat trousers, a long sleeved cotton t-shirt, a jumper, a pair of socks, boxer shorts, and a pair of sturdy boots. Each item was navy blue. There was a label on the left sleeve of both the jumper and the t-shirt. Julius grinned with pride as he read the silver letters: 'Julius McCoy – 1MJ – Tijara School'. He was about to remove his own jumper when a sudden thought made him stop – would Faith need help getting changed? And how was he supposed to ask without embarrassing him in front of the others?

Unfortunately, Somers seemed to have had the same thought and was now turning towards Faith. 'Shanigan, do you want me to call that nice lady to help you out?' he asked with a sneer.

Julius froze, unable to believe what he had just heard. He knew that kids often mocked each other for a laugh, but in certain cases you just didn't. It was a line no one with even a hint of decency would ever cross. For that reason, the changing room had suddenly gone quiet and all eyes were fixed on Billy and Faith.

'Thank you Somers,' said Faith, smiling suddenly. 'But I'm already waiting for your sister.'

Somers's face turned danger-red and he advanced towards Faith, fists clenched. Julius and Alan Cross immediately jumped between them.

'Let me at him!' cried Somers, trying to remove Cross from his path.

'Yeah, let him come!' shouted Faith, waving his fists in the air.

'He insulted my sister!'

'That's 'cause you insulted him first!' shouted back Julius, trying to keep Faith's chair from advancing.

At that moment, an angry female voice bellowed out from a speaker in the room: 'If I hear another sound coming from that room, none of you gentlemen will leave this Zed Centre. Ever!'

Julius felt Faith's chair stop, and released his hold. Somers threw Faith a nasty look and went back to his bench.

'I don't need help,' said Faith, his cheeks now slightly flushed. With that, he turned around and started to undress.

Julius did likewise, but kept glancing towards Faith to check that he really could do it by himself. To his surprise, he did so very smoothly. His chair had special in-built arms that could lift Faith's body and legs while he changed his trousers.

Once ready, Julius folded his old clothes and placed them inside the grey pack. There was a mirror in the room and, when Julius caught sight of his reflection, he instantly knew that this uniform was the symbol of a new life. Julius and Faith both had navy blue uniforms. Alan Cross's was dark red and Billy Somers's was olive green. They went back to the waiting room where the girls were already waiting. Morgana's uniform was also navy blue, but under the jumper she was wearing a pleated, knee-length skirt and a pair of tall leather boots with flat heels.

The grey-uniformed woman threw a hard look at the boys. 'Everyone follow me now,' she said sternly and led them out of the room past the reception desk.

Crossing over the paved square, they walked past the visitor's building where their parents had waited for them during their test, and arrived at a runway. There, a small white shuttle was waiting for them. It was perched on three wheels, with a set of steps leading to an opening in its side.

The rain was still lashing down so everybody ran to the steps, covering their heads with their rucksacks. Faith waited behind for the others to embark, and then hovered directly inside.

Once aboard, they were told to sit near the front. Faith moved over to the designated area, where he locked his chair in place. The woman checked that all their seatbelts were fastened while the shuttle prepared for takeoff. Julius looked out of the window to see if the Bumble Bee was still there but the rain was too heavy to make anything out. The shuttle engines hummed into life and several minutes later they were airborne.

The flight to Prague was only thirty minutes long. Julius watched the landscape rolling by quickly, with Morgana's head resting on his shoulder. Below him, he saw other vehicles criss-crossing in the air and knew that none of them were allowed to fly anywhere near their Zed shuttle. When Julius was eight, Mr McCoy had explained to him that there were three different flying systems in the world. The lower one was used by fly-cars; the second system, at a higher altitude, was for private aircraft and fly-buses; the third one, an exclusive, high-speed system, was only to be used by Zed personnel. Any trespassers risked being sucked into the jet-stream of the fastest aircrafts on Earth, and if they were still alive after that and had no good reason for trespassing in the first place, being deported to the infamous Halls of Ahriman. Mr McCoy had not been too sure about where Ahriman was or where it had gained its reputation from, but the general opinion was that it was a doomed place and for the young Julius it was enough to decide that he would never trespass in the Zed high-speed system.

They were flying over the German border when the pilot announced that they would be landing in the next few minutes. Morgana leaned over Julius to look down. It was a beautiful sunny day and they could see Prague below with the river Vltava dividing the city into two halves.

'Look, that's Charles Bridge, and that one is Prague Castle,' said Julius.

They watched the west side of the city passing by, while the shuttle slowly descended towards the Zed departure centre. Upon landing, the aircraft kept moving along the runway and disappeared inside a tunnel. When it finally came to a halt, the woman led them all out.

The departure centre was a large hall with metal walls and a stained glass roof. Sunrays were streaming through its glass panels, creating beautiful rainbows on the floor below. Julius saw several doors leading out from the main area, some marked "ZED PERSONNEL ONLY" and others "CIVILIAN PERSONNEL ONLY". There was also a café, lit up in purple neon, and a number of world restaurants. The main hall was crawling with boys and girls of all nationalities. Julius saw that in the middle of the hall, hovering in mid-air, there were three silver signs. Each of them represented one of the three Zed schools. Below each sign, three squared sectors had been created with metal rails to gather the respective students. Julius's group followed the woman with the grey uniform through the noisy crowd. She stopped before a small gate, behind which was Tijara's sector. A tall officer, wearing a Tijaran uniform, took three microchips from the woman and ushered Julius, Morgana and Faith inside.

'See you in Satras,' said Morgana, waving to the girls.

'Bye Julius. Bye Faith,' Alan Cross called after them.

'Yes, Shanigan, see you later,' added Somers sarcastically.

The woman pushed Somers forward unceremoniously before Faith could reply.

'What was that about?' asked Morgana, holding the gate open for Faith. She suddenly heard Julius's voice in her head: *'Somers has been on his back ever since last spring, and Faith has his own wonderful way of dealing with provocation.'* He then gave her a quick summary of that morning's skirmish in the changing room. Morgana shook her head and muttered something about boys and brains.

When they entered the sector, a few smiling faces turned towards them.

Julius, Faith and Morgana smiled back and moved towards the side of the perimeter.

'There must be about sixty of us in all the sectors and more are coming out from the aircrafts,' said Faith, hovering high above their heads, until the Tijaran officer told him to land immediately.

Twenty minutes later, they heard the officer talking into an earpiece, confirming that his students were all present. Julius looked around him and counted 30 people in his group. He was curious to know where they were all from but knew better than to browse around in other people's minds. His parents had taught him very early in life about the importance of freedom and privacy. 'How would you like it if Morgana knew all your secrets and told them to your friends?' Mr McCoy had asked him. Julius had blushed furiously at the thought and since then had tried very hard to not take his skills lightly. However, there were occasional moments in which he could unintentionally perceive other people's thoughts, especially when he was relaxed, and that made him very uncomfortable.

Slowly, the area between the sectors and the runway cleared. All the students were inside the perimeters and Julius watched as the Tijaran officer joined them and locked the gate behind him. Suddenly, the platform on which they were standing began to descend through the floor. Julius grabbed hold of the rail to steady himself and Morgana held on to Faith's chair. He felt the platform changing direction several times as it followed its underground track before coming to a halt in front of a wall where a single door stood. The officer spoke again into his earpiece and the door opened. He then turned towards the students.

'My name is Captain Foster. I am in charge of Tijara's security. Every year I volunteer to collect the new students from Earth so that I have the chance to memorise each and every face. Make sure you do not have reason to meet me again, except for official receptions ... or war.' He paused and fixed them all with an icy look.

Julius thought that his voice alone had been enough to carry his point home, even without the killer stare, but obviously he wasn't going to bring that up.

'Once through this door,' continued Foster, 'you will be inside the Zed shuttle. I want you to occupy seats one to thirty. Lift off is at 10:00 hours. In two hours, you will be in Zed. Shanigan, you go first. Move it!'

The group parted quickly to let Faith pass, and Julius and Morgana followed him. They entered from a side door near the front of the shuttle. There were two long rows of seats, three-by-three, divided by a corridor. To his left, Julius saw the other students embarking, the Tuala group in the centre and the Sields at the back. Faith moved to the top of the left row and locked his chair in place. Julius and Morgana took the seats behind him, leaving an empty one near the corridor.

'I'm glad there has been some progress in gravity research,' said Julius, fastening his seatbelt. 'Can you imagine travelling to the Moon in one of those ancient rockets?'

'Aye, it must have been murder,' said Morgana, examining the shuttle. 'These models look just like normal aircrafts, but the magic is in the engines.'

'As always,' said Faith. 'However, I would improve it with a touch or two, starting with the thrusters setup that is ...'

At that moment, a boy walked up to them. He had a bush of brown curly hair and a dark tan.

'*Aloha*, mind if I sit here?' he asked, smiling.

'Not at all,' said Morgana, who as always was the first to socialise with strangers. '*Konnichiwa!*'

'Wow! Was that Japanese?' asked the boy.

'Yes it was. But it's easier if we keep using the common speech. I'm Morgana. These two are Julius and Faith.'

'I'm Lopaka Liway, from Hawaii. Good to meet you!'

'Hawaii?' cried Faith. 'Do you surf by any chance?'

'Even when I sleep,' replied Lopaka.

'Then you are me man. Come, sit. We have much to discuss,' said Faith, excitedly.

Julius and Morgana looked at each other, puzzled. Even Lopaka appeared to be surprised but, since he clearly loved the sport so much, he was more than happy to pass the time discussing waves, waxes and boards.

When the shuttle lifted off, Julius barely noticed it, but he knew that he was rising above the clouds and making a straight line for the stars. The idea that he was leaving the Earth's orbit was slowly sinking in and he felt a new wave of excitement rushing through his body. He was happy to be there, happy to be alive and even ashamedly happy that there had been a Chemical War, since it was the only reason he was now on his way to the Moon.

As Morgana had gone to meet some of the girls behind them, Julius joined Faith and Lopaka in their surfing chat. They had been flying for over an hour when Morgana came back and dropped herself into her seat with a big smile on her face.

'I've met some of the girls in our class,' she explained happily to Julius. 'Many of them come from the colonies and they were telling me all about it. Maybe one day we'll be able to visit them. Wouldn't that be great?'

'And maybe you'll be piloting the ship that takes us there.'

'One day I will. Right now though, I want to watch this Zed video with you. When I went to visit Kaori before, it wasn't on our shuttle. Put on your headphones.' Morgana pushed a button on the armrest of her chair and a holoscreen appeared in front of them. She put on her own headphones and plugged Julius's in next to hers. A few seconds later, the head of a young pretty woman with a blonde bob appeared on the screen.

'Good morning, and welcome to space! Please select the topic of interest from the choices below.'

Three touch-pads appeared over her smiling face: 'Moon', 'Marcus Tijara' and 'Zed Lunar Perimeter'. Morgana touched the first one and the screen faded slowly to black. As different pictures of the Moon started to scroll past, the lady's voice told them all sorts of information. Julius knew most of the things she was telling them about but he did manage to learn some new facts.

'As seen from the Earth, the Moon appears to have bright and dark patches – the bright ones are craters and mountains which can catch the Sun's light, and the dark ones are low-lying plains. Centuries ago, those plains were thought to be seas, or *mária*, and today we still call them by their first given names, such as Sea of Rains or Ocean of Storms, although in truth the Moon is entirely without water.

'The Moon does not have atmosphere, which means several things: the edges of the shadows are sharp as razors, since there is no mist to make them softer; there is no sound, since this needs air to travel; there is no protection from the Sun during the day and no way to imprison heat during the night, creating great extremes of temperature. Along the Equator, the daily temperature is 100 degrees Celsius, whereas the night temperature can fall to -160 degrees.'

'Whoa,' cried Julius. 'That's almost as low as liquid air!'

'Well, I'm not planning any trekking outside the Lunar Perimeter,' added Morgana quickly.

'Let's hear about Marcus Tijara,' said Julius, touching the screen. The woman's smiling face reappeared and so did the three options. He pressed the next button and the screen faded once more to be replaced by the face of Marcus Tijara.

'Marcus Tijara was the first scientist to research the effects caused by the Chemical War of the 25th century. Tijara himself was granted the gift, or curse as some would call it, of highly developed mind-skills. By 2620, Tijara, who had become highly esteemed in the eyes of the Earth Leader, was granted permission to build the Zed Lunar Perimeter on the Moon. The Perimeter was to become home to the Curia and to the Zed Academy, a base for exploration of the galaxy and a defence system to maintain the hard won peace on planet Earth.' The blurb finished and the main menu reappeared.

'Is that all?' asked Julius, disappointed. 'I thought she was going to tell us about Marcus's battle with Clodagh Arnesh, and of how they both died.'

'We'll probably study that in class.'

Julius pressed the last button.

'This is the Zed Lunar Perimeter,' said the woman. 'Only Zed Members and Curia personnel are allowed to live in the Perimeter. Students of the schools are given special permission to reside in Zed until completion of their six years of training, which will qualify them as Zed Members. They will study for two years as Mizki Juniors, two years as Apprentices and two years as Seniors. The only habitable lunar area, Zed has been developed across four low-plains. As you can see from the picture, the plain at the top is the Sea of Serenity, where you will find the Zed Docks. Below it is the Sea of Tranquillity, where you can relax in the bustling and friendly Satras. Who said that the Moon doesn't have atmosphere?' added the voice with a giggle.

'I can't believe she said that,' said Julius, in a deadpan voice.

'She did, she did,' added Morgana, equally serious.

'... Just to the right of the Sea of Tranquillity,' continued the woman, 'we have the Sea of Fertility, where the Zed schools are situated: Tuala, Sield and of course Tijara, where Marcus himself was Grand Master. In the schools, selected students can develop their mind-skills in the form of White and Grey Arts. Finally, the plain at the bottom is the Sea of Nectar, home to the Curia, where the headquarters of Colonial Affairs are located.'

The woman's head flashed up for the last time, 'If you require any further information, visit us in Satras, at the information kiosk. Thank you for your attention and, once again, welcome to Zed,' she said, as the holoscreen disappeared.

'It's all so exciting,' said Morgana, putting their headsets away.

'Learned anything new?' asked Faith, now that they had finished.

'Yeah. The lady here recommended going for a walk outside Zed around midday,' said Julius.

Faith looked a bit puzzled, but Morgana shook her head and rolled her eyes. 'Don't listen to him. She didn't say that. However, she *did* say some interesting stuff.' Morgana then promptly filled Faith in on her latest discoveries.

Ten minutes later, a voice came through the speakers which were fitted above each row. 'All students return to their seats immediately and fasten their seatbelts for landing.'

Excited murmurs spread through the shuttle as everyone ran back to their seats. Unfortunately, he couldn't see much through the small windows, so Julius had to be content with sitting back comfortably, closing his eyes and imagining his very first landing on the Moon.

A NEW HOME

The shuttle came to a halt at the Zed Docks at 12:00 hours. The students were so excited that half of them threw off their seatbelts the instant they landed. Captain Foster, who was in charge of the Tijaran students, stood in the middle of their section with his hands behind his back. A single glance from him was all it took to get everybody's attention.

'We are about to board the Zed Intra-Rail system,' he said. 'It will take us to Tijara. Where I go, you go. Keep your eyes on me at all times and don't make me come and find you. I also strongly recommend that you practice your school's salute.'

Julius threw a worried look at Morgana, because he couldn't remember what the salute was. By the look in her eyes, it was clear that she wasn't going to be much help.

'Have either of you two actually read that chip?' asked Faith with a theatrical sigh. 'What are you like. Come on, I'll show you what to do once we get on the train.'

The students poured into the corridor and Julius let Morgana and Faith go ahead of him. The shuttle door opened onto a platform inside a brightly lit gallery, where the train was already waiting.

'Shame, I thought we would land in the centre of our own docks,' said Morgana, disappointed. 'This is where any old visitor from Earth lands.'

Julius looked to his right, where a metallic gate blocked the tunnel. Behind it, he thought with excitement, were all the spaceships that he would soon be flying. He had just enough time to see the other schools' students boarding the two train compartments behind his own, before he was dragged inside by Morgana.

'I feel like I'm inside a suppository,' said Faith looking around, and indeed the train carriages did have that exact shape. With the exception of the metallic floor, the three sections were completely made of glass, no doubt to give a better view on the journey.

The train left the tunnel and made its way out of the Sea of Serenity. Not one of the students uttered a word; they were too busy staring all around them, mouths gaping in wonder. Julius wasn't sure that his brain was actually registering where he was. The surface of the Moon was bright grey and interrupted by small ridges, gaps and channels – the old scars left behind by the meteorites that had collided with it eons ago.

'Look above you, guys. That shield is the coolest of all! I wish I had invented it,' exclaimed Faith.

Julius and Morgana looked up as Faith enthusiastically imparted his technical wisdom on them. 'See, the shield recreates Earth's atmosphere and covers the whole of Zed. Not only does it block out the sunlight, which would turn us into toast otherwise, but it's also the reason why we can breathe and why we have gravity … and see those little dots there, and there and … anyway, that's the illumination system. It gives us night and day as we'd have on Earth and keeps the temperature constantly mild.'

Julius noticed that Morgana was listening to this description in a sort of trance, as if Faith had been describing a succulent fudge cake. He smiled knowingly – for Morgana, technological wonders were as tasty as honey was to bears.

'That's really great, Faith, but now show us that salute thingy,' said Julius, lowering his voice and checking that nobody was listening.

'Oh, it's quite simple really. You place your right fist on your heart, or was it the left … no wait …'

'Faith,' cut in Julius, 'can you visualise what you saw in that chip?'

'Sure. Why?'

'I'll try to break in.'

'You what?' said Faith, sounding very worried.

'You won't feel a thing, promise. Just close your eyes. Morgana, give me your hand. You too, Faith. On three. One … two … three!' Julius closed his eyes.

From the darkness, a familiar single point of light emerged, growing slowly into a tunnel. Julius projected the tunnel mentally forward until he came across Morgana's mind-link. He joined it to his own and together they shot forward into Faith's mind. There, an image began to form: hundreds of people stood in orderly rows. Julius concentrated on a boy at the front. His right arm was pressed against his body, fist clenched, while the other hand rested on the shoulder of the person to his left. A voice cried, "In your heart!" and everyone shouted back, "Tijara!". Julius saw that on pronouncing the last syllable, the boy slammed his right fist against his heart and stamped his right foot on the ground. Then the image faded and he drew back from Faith.

'I got goose bumps,' said Morgana. 'That looked positively … charging.'

'I got goose bumps too,' said Faith, 'but only because I feel violated! It's incredible that you can do that, Julius. Just remember to ask first, all right?'

When the train approached Satras station, it didn't stop, but turned left towards the Sea of Fertility, where the schools awaited. Slightly puzzled, Julius watched as Morgana started to climb the back of Faith's chair.

'Can you fly up a bit, Faith?' she asked, tapping him on the shoulder. 'I want to see if I can spot Tijara.'

'You'll bang your head on the ceiling, woman!' said Faith, hovering upwards.

'There it is! I see it. It's soooo beautiful,' cried Morgana with her hands and nose pressed against the glass roof. At those words, the other students turned to the left and let out a gasp as Tijara appeared from behind a bend.

An outer wall of sandstone surrounded a tall glass dome, whose upper portion touched the Zed shield and merged with it. From the top of the dome, water slid down the glass and fell in gentle waterfalls over the sandstone walls, ending in a placid moat that surrounded the school, making it appear as if it was on an island. Embedded in the wall were large stained glass windows, framed by luscious tropical plants and multi coloured flowers which stretched towards the sky. The reflections created by the artificial light as they bounced off the water made the school glow like an oasis in the middle of a desert.

Julius turned around just in time to see Captain Foster watching the students, a rare little smile on his face. Then he straightened up and resumed his usual seriousness.

'Tijaran students, time to get your bags, double quick! Miss Ruthier,' he said looking at Morgana. 'I think you've trespassed enough on Mr Shanigan's hospitality.'

Morgana leapt off Faith's chair onto the floor, almost landing on a boy who was standing nearby. The boy steadied her and smiled. She looked into his green eyes and Julius noticed her turning very red indeed. He also saw something else – a faint wisp of pink rising above her head. Julius had seen wisps like that before; he had long since figured that they must be emotions and generally that was his cue to look away because, when people displayed their feelings so strongly, it was easier for him to look into their minds.

When the train came to a halt, he shouldered his rucksack and followed as the Tijaran students stepped out onto the platform.

'Are you sure we're not in the Caribbean?' asked Faith, stretching his arms contentedly.

After hours spent cooped up inside buildings and shuttles, Julius was loving the warmth of the air on his skin. The rain of Scotland, which only that morning had soaked through his clothes, was already a distant memory.

The platform led them towards the main gate of Tijara, creating a bridge over the moat, which was protected from the waterfalls by large sheets of glass. Captain Foster ordered them into a single line and ushered them inside one by one through a small barrier on the right side of the entrance. When Julius's turn arrived, the Captain told him to look left into a dark, square gap. He saw a red dot and knew that his retinas were being scanned. There was a beeping noise and the barrier opened. He moved forward into the reception area, where a man in a grey uniform was gathering the students in front of a glass door. His badge read "James Leven, Front Gate Guard". To the left of the barrier Julius saw a waiting room furnished with sofas and armchairs. It was a pleasant area where the light streamed through stained glass windows, creating a warm atmosphere. Behind the sofas, a staircase disappeared into the floor. Above it, a sign read "TIJARA – HANGAR ACCESS".

'That'll be my bedroom then!' said Morgana, pointing at it.

'You should get them to change the sign then. For privacy, you know,' added Faith.

At that moment, Captain Foster brushed past them and touched a button to the left of the door, which slid open noiselessly. They stepped into a large circular promenade, tiled in white marble. Potted plants stood between sliding glass doors, which opened at regular intervals along the perimeter. In the centre of the promenade, a black cylindrical structure rose all the way up to the ceiling. At the point where it merged with the dome, water trickled down over its slick surface, creating an encircling pool at its base, which was lined with benches. The double doors of this inner structure opened as they approached, and Foster ushered them inside.

The brightness that had accompanied them throughout Zed disappeared unexpectedly and it took a few seconds for Julius to adjust to the dim light of the hall. Ahead of him, he could see a raised podium with a handful of seats behind it while the rest of the hall was occupied by rows of chairs, facing towards it.

Foster motioned for them to sit at the front. Julius and Morgana did so, deliberately choosing seats at the end of the first row, so that Faith could stop next to them. When everyone was settled, they heard a noise above their heads and watched in astonishment as the ceiling parted, revealing the black and starry sky beyond the Zed shield.

'Welcome to space,' said a voice suddenly.

All heads turned towards the stage, where the Grand Master of Tijara stood. Julius recognised Carlos Freja immediately from the portrait he

45

had seen in the Test Centre. If the man in the picture had produced a sense of admiration in Julius, the real one made him want to hide behind his seat, for the sheer intensity of his grey eyes alone. Every bit of Freja screamed order and discipline: his short hair, his pristine blue uniform, his posture. Even his voice had sounded powerful without being overly loud. Julius watched, enraptured as Freja scanned the students with his piercing eyes and, when they came to rest upon him, he could have sworn that they had widened imperceptibly. Gradually, the Grand Master let his face relax a little, and the faintest hint of a smile appeared on his lips. Julius heard Morgana, and several others behind him, let out a sigh of relief at this change.

'I trust your journey has been pleasant. Judging by Captain Foster's report, I believe you were all pleased at the sight of Tijara.' As he said this, he looked towards Morgana and Faith with an eyebrow raised and Julius saw his friends blushing wildly.

'Tijara is the soul of Zed,' continued Freja, 'the first creation of Marcus Tijara on this incredible satellite that is the Moon. And Zed is a gift, born from the mistakes of mankind, for the salvation of mankind. It is a reminder of how low we humans can sink, and of how high we can rise when we set our hearts to following their true path: that of defending the greatest gift of all – life.

'Only thirty of you stand before me today, the thirty most gifted 12 year-olds that Earth and its colonies have to offer. Wear your pride upon your face, for you will carry the traditions of Zed forward. And at the same time, coat your heart with humility, for the journey of life is long and your learning will never end.'

As Freja's words were still lingering in the air, Nathan Cress walked up the central aisle and stopped under the podium, where he turned to face the students.

'Mizki, stand for the salute,' he ordered, standing to attention.

Julius scrambled to his feet along with the others. He put his right arm at his side and his left hand on Faith's shoulder.

'In your heart!' cried Freja.

'TI-JA-RA!' they cried back in unison. As the echo of their voices and stamping feet faded, Julius felt a rush of energy shooting through his body. For the first time since his test, the reality of his new life struck him fully, and he felt tears of pride swelling in his eyes.

Freja nodded, impressed, and left the hall.

'All female students,' said Cress, 'make your way to the promenade and follow Miss Child to your dorms.'

'See you later, guys,' said Morgana, grabbing her bag.

Once the girls had left, Cress got the boys moving too. Waiting outside was an older boy wearing a well pressed uniform and sporting a sharply cropped hairstyle. Julius looked at the label on his left sleeve and saw that he was a final year student, a 6 Mizki Senior, named Tony Tower. He asked them to follow him and then set off. They headed off to the right and walked past a door, which a sign identified as the staff quarters. The boys' dorm was the one after, followed by the girls'. Tower led them on and stopped in a small atrium.

'Each dorm has six underground floors – lift or stairs, it's up to you. Each year has its floor: the first years sleep on level -6. Every room is shared by two students. You'll find your names on the door tags. To open the door, look into the keyhole – it has a sensor that scans your retina. Every security door in Zed works like this and, if you are authorised to enter, it will open. You can make your way down now to leave your bags. You will need to report to the mess hall at 14:00 for lunch. Do not be late.'

As Tower left them, Julius stepped into one of the four lifts with

Faith and a few of the other students. When they reached their floor, they found themselves at the beginning of a long bright corridor, with doors to either side. At the end of it, a blue sky could be seen through a large window.

'Aren't we underground?' asked Julius, perplexed.

'It's probably one of those funky scenery screens. Anyway, this is me room right he-'

At that moment, a muffled voice called out for help from inside the room. Faith looked into the scanner quickly and the door opened. Julius stepped back, startled by the sight that greeted him. Partition walls inside the room were sliding back and forth, out of control. Beds and chairs were appearing and disappearing from holes in the floor, while various computer screens were flipping frantically through the side walls. A small boy was stuck in the bathroom at the far end of the room, a look of total panic on his face.

'Press the red button near the door. Make it stop, please!' cried the boy.

Julius, being careful not to get squashed in between the partition walls, reached out his arm to the control panel and slammed his hand against the red button. Everything stopped and all the partitions slid back into place.

'That was close,' said the boy, walking towards them.

'Are you ok?' asked Julius, trying not to laugh.

'Yeah, sorry about that ... must have pressed the wrong combination ... I'm Bartholomeus Smit – Barth if you please, from Holland.'

'I'm Faith, your Irish roommate. This is Julius McCoy from Scotland.'

'Nice meeting you, and thanks for ... you know ...'

'No worries, but we should try to get this room sussed before we go to bed,' said Faith with a grin.

'You do that. I'll go find my room,' said Julius, leaving Barth and Faith on the threshold cautiously pressing various buttons.

Julius's room was the third on the right. The name "Skye Miller" was written underneath his. He looked into the keyhole and the door slid open. His new roommate was already there, emptying the contents of his rucksack into the drawers of his desk. Julius recognised him from the train as the one who Morgana had landed on earlier. He had messy blonde hair and green eyes. Julius felt a good vibe coming from him and smiled involuntarily. It didn't happen often, but when it did it was always a good sign. As he walked in, the boy stood up and stretched his hand out.

'How's it going? I'm Skye.'

'Julius. Nice to meet you.'

'Hope you don't mind if I sleep on this side.'

'Not at all. Did you figure out the controls?'

'Sure. Come here in the corner and I'll show you.'

They moved over to the control panel next to the door and Skye pressed the red reset button. His desk disappeared into the wall, leaving the room completely empty.

'This is the starting stage,' said Skye. 'See here, there are two rows of buttons, one for you and one for me. When you press the first button, the partitions come up creating two distinct areas, which are our rooms. Then the second button gets the beds up from the floor. The ceiling is actually a scenery screen, so you can sleep under a starry sky if you like.'

As Skye pushed the second button, Julius entered inside his own area.

'There's a drawer at the bottom of the bed for your clothes,' explained Skye.

Julius opened it and saw that there were two sections.

'It says here to put your dirty clothes on the right,' he said.

'They probably get picked up by someone when the bed is back in the floor,' said Skye. 'Anyway, step away from the bed. The third button opens a section in the wall where your desk and computer terminal are stored. And finally, this last button is definitely my favourite.'

Julius leapt backwards as a large reclining chair came up from the floor while a multi-purpose screen flipped out from the wall.

'This is just!' cried Julius.

Skye joined him inside his space. 'Neat, huh? And once the partitions are up, you can change your room from the inside,' he said, pointing to a small panel on the wall.

At that moment, there was a knock at the door. Julius opened it and Faith hovered inside.

'Is this room something or what?' asked Faith.

'For sure! Hey Faith, this is Skye.'

'Hi. Nice chair, mate,' said Skye, shaking Faith's hand.

'Thanks. I'm quite proud of it you know. Built it all by meself.'

'Faith is very technical,' added Julius.

'Indeed I am, but I'm also famished. Shall we go up?'

They all readily agreed and made their way up to the promenade. With the exception of the other first year students, the place was empty. They walked past the girls' dorm and quickly checked the lounge, a vast room with sofas and tables, and a large fireplace. At the mess hall entrance, Tower was handing out booklets to the students as they walked past him. Julius rolled his up, put it in one of his trouser leg pockets and joined the queue for the food.

The mess hall was a huge area filled with artificial sunlight from the shield. Ten long tables occupied the right hand side, and on the left a food counter separated the hall from the kitchen. Julius could see at least five cooks dishing out mouth-watering platters at incredible speed. To the back of the hall, a glass door opened into what looked like a small garden. Julius could make out trees, benches and even a stream, winding its way around various pathways.

'That looks positively girly …' said Faith, who was looking in the same direction.

Julius nodded. He was sure that Morgana would be quite delighted to spend her free time in there.

Above the tables, mounted against the far wall, was a large screen with messages and name charts scrolling across it. At the top of the screen, the word "Hologram Palace" flashed in bright red letters.

'Look at that, guys!' cried Julius. 'It shows all the top scores from the Satras games.'

'Me name will be there soon,' said Faith.

'And you can check results by school, by team and by individual as well,' added Skye. 'Shame that we aren't allowed on Satras until next month.'

They each grabbed a tray of food, sat down at one of the tables and started reading their booklets. Inside was a black and white map of Zed and another of Tijara. Julius saw that the infirmary was next to the mess hall, followed by the library, the holographic sector, the classrooms for the White and Grey Arts, and the offices. Every sector went deep underground, like the dorms. The booklet also contained information on the Fyver, the official currency of Zed. It said that, at the end of each week, students would receive up to ten Fyvers that could be spent in Satras, and that the amount gained was tied to how well the student performed during that week.

'Outstanding students,' said Faith in a solemn voice, 'will receive commendations in their files, but act like Billy Somers and you'll get expelled.'

'Who's Somers?' asked Skye.

'A stuck-up nasty number, all the way from the sewers of Earth.'

'He's at Sield,' added Julius, relieved.

Faith continued his scan of the booklet aloud until he found a paragraph on personal conduct: 'Always preserve the school's reputation and remember rule number one, be very careful and thoughtful if ...'

'If what, Faith?' asked Julius, chewing his grilled halloumi salad with gusto.

'... if you decide to start a relationship,' finished Faith, almost in a whisper.

After a few seconds of general silence, Julius swallowed.

'As if ...' he said, looking quickly away.

'Yeah,' butted in Faith even more quickly, 'that's girl's stuff!'

At the end of the meal, Julius placed his empty tray on a trolley and saw Morgana waving to him from the garden.

'Did you eat outside?' asked Julius, sitting down on the grass beside her.

'It's so beautiful here. The sun, the sound of the water, the smell of the trees. I love it!' said Morgana lying down.

'I thought you would.'

Faith and Skye joined them and Faith introduced their new friend to her. Julius saw that Morgana had recognised him from the train, but was relieved to notice that there was no pink wisp above her head this time. He had to admit that the garden was really relaxing and, as all the other students were there too, they spent the entire afternoon lying on the grass, talking and laughing. Thanks to Morgana's friendliness, they also managed to meet most of the students from their year and, when they went back into the mess hall to eat their supper, Julius's table was awash with new faces.

Faith had discovered that Skye liked surfing too, and together they had cornered Lopaka Liway into sharing techniques with them over a crème brûlée. Julius was deep in conversation with a Hungarian boy called Ferenc Orbán who, like him, had a real passion for history. Only when they had discussed the most important monarchs, rulers and dictators of Hungarian history – 'My favourite is Matthias "The Raven"'– 'Agreed. He's the coolest.'– 'What about Zsigmond?' – ' Yeah, but he didn't stop the Ottomans.' – did they feel satisfied and ready to go to sleep.

As he lay on his new bed that night, Julius watched the Milky Way drift past on his scenery screen. His mind was so full of the things he had seen that day, and of the people he had met, that it took him a while to wind down. Eventually his eyes closed and he fell asleep with a big smile on his face.

LIFE IN TIJARA

At seven o'clock, a violent alarm sound woke the entire floor up. A loud voice called for the students to get dressed and lined up in the corridor in three minutes. Julius awoke with a jolt, leapt out of his bed and ran from his area, colliding with Skye in front of their bathroom.

'Where am I? Who are you?' blurted out Skye, his eyes still half closed.

It took them a few seconds to realise what was going on and to retreat hastily back into their areas. Julius grabbed his clothes and ran into the corridor, hoping sincerely that it wasn't going to be like this every morning for the next six years. Outside, Tony Tower was standing by the lift waiting for them.

'Good morning gentlemen. Glad to see you are all present,' he said, looking up and down the two rows of students. Julius did likewise and noticed that yes, they were all present, but most of them were also half naked, except for Faith, who looked as neat and pristine as Tower did.

'From tomorrow,' continued Tower, 'you will be able to set your own alarm, but if one of you is ever late for class, the whole floor will lose that privilege for a week. Breakfast is between 07:00 and 08:30

54

and you must be INSIDE the class by 09:00. When we greet a teacher or a superior in general, we bow our heads as a sign of respect; they will bow to you in return. Get dressed now, *properly*, and make your way to the mess hall. There I shall hand out your timetables.'

Tower bowed his head slightly and they all bowed back. When Julius got to the mess hall he saw that it was teeming with older students – they had all returned for the start of the new school year. He found Faith and Morgana, sitting at one of the tables, already eating.

'Morning lot,' he said sitting down. 'Did you girls get the alarm from hell too?'

'Aye. You should have seen us: hair everywhere, boots in hands and blurry eyes ... not charming.'

'Same here ... except for Shanigan.'

'I was already awake,' said Faith defensively. 'I didn't know what time we were supposed to be up, and since it takes me a while ... but do not fear! In case of emergency, I shall fight in nothing but me underwear.'

'That's the spirit!' said Skye, joining them. 'Here, these are the timetables.'

Julius grabbed his with excitement but that didn't last long.

'Three hours of Meditation on a Monday morning? You've got to be kidding me!' he said, distressed. '*And* we have to write diary entries for all of the subjects ...'

'Telekinesis and ... what the heck is Draw?' asked Faith.

'Three hours of Spaceology on a Wednesday morning ...' echoed Skye feebly.

'At least it's followed by Martial Arts. And on Friday it's all Pilot Training!' said Morgana excitedly.

That last bit of news was good enough for them, and when they left the mess hall they were in a much cheerier mood.

At 08:40, they made their way to the holographic sector where a man in a Tijaran uniform, by the name of Gabriel List, told them to go one floor down to room one. This area was large and completely white, with no chairs or desks. The students walked in uncertainly, as if they were expecting the whole place to suddenly disappear. The floor seemed to be made of glass, and Julius found himself probing it with his foot to make sure it was thick enough to support their weight.

'It will hold, Mr McCoy, do not worry,' said a kindly voice from behind him.

Julius turned and saw an old Chinese man standing by the door. His head was completely bald, but a thin white goatee reached to his chest. He wore a loose tunic over baggy trousers and a pair of training slippers. Every item of his clothing was as white as his goatee. The man knelt down on the floor and with his arms he gestured for the students to do likewise, in a semi circle around him. He then bowed his head to them and the students bowed back.

'I am Professor Len Lao-tzu,' he said. His voice was calm and well paced, his face relaxed. 'Can one of you tell me your definition of Meditation?'

After a brief nervous silence, a boy put his hand up. Julius had met him the day before – Dumisai Chiddy, from Zimbabwe.

'Sir, is a state of contemplation ... Sir.'

'Very good. Any additions to that?'

'Sir,' said Morgana, 'a state of extended reflection or contemplation.'

'Thank you Miss Ruthier. Indeed, reflecting or contemplating for extended periods of time is what we practice in Meditation. There are good reasons for it, obviously. In a meditative state, the body consumes less oxygen and expends less energy. Your brain pattern will show mainly alpha waves: they are the electrical activity of one who is awake, but relaxed.

'In this school, you will learn to develop and control the White Arts. Meditation, being the most basic of them, is also the means to do just that. Being able to relax your mind at will allows you to perform under pressure. This brings us to your aim for this year – to master this art in order to achieve a perfect state of relaxation in less than one minute.'

Lao-tzu stood and asked the students to rise and line up along the walls. Julius heard a buzzing noise coming from under his feet and suddenly the floor split into several different panels, each one large enough for a person to lie on.

'As you can see there are a number of scenery screens on the floor. I would like you to choose the one that best brings forth a feeling of relaxation in you. Then sit on it and wait for the others,' said Lao-tzu.

Julius scanned the floor quickly. There were many country settings, with and without sheep; there was one completely black panel and another with only water. In the far right corner of the room he finally saw one that he liked and moved towards it. It showed a solitary, stony tower rising from the top of a hill towards the night sky. Julius sat down and looked around. Next to him, Skye had chosen the water picture and was watching the fishes swimming below him. Morgana – 'Very predictable,' thought Julius – was sitting on a picture of a forest clearing, with a stream cutting through it and a cloud of butterflies flitting in and out of view. He noticed that Faith's picture was a single fluffy cloud against a blue sky.

'Now that you are all settled,' said Lao-tzu, 'place your finger on the spot where you would like to land. As it is your first time in a holographic environment of this kind, I recommend you close your eyes during the activation – it could be somewhat disorientating.'

He clapped his hands once and each screen, and its occupant, became instantly enveloped in what looked like a soap bubble. Excited, Julius placed his finger on the top of the tower and closed his eyes. Suddenly, he felt a gush of fresh air in his face and, as all other noises faded into the distance, he found himself enveloped by the stillness of the night. Lao-tzu's soothing voice came to him and he opened his eyes.

'Breathe deeply, slowly. Clear your mind of everything and let the night embrace you.'

Julius measured his breathing and focused on a distant point in front of him. After a few minutes though, he realised that it wasn't working at all. He couldn't get his mind to relax, full as it was with all that had happened in the last two days. He tried closing his eyes, he tried lying down, he even tried standing up, but with no success – the night wasn't coming anywhere near him.

'That's great,' he muttered, sitting down again. The thought of spending the next three hours perched on that tower like a vulture made him quite depressed. Eventually he lay down and, without realising it, drifted into sleep. When he opened his eyes again, he saw that he was back in the room. He sat up, embarrassed, but quickly noticed that all of his classmates were also asleep. Faith's head was lolling to one side, while Skye was snoring profoundly next to him. Professor Lao-tzu was sitting facing them, and when Julius met his eyes he felt himself blushing.

'Sorry Professor,' he managed to mumble in the direction of his teacher.

Lao-tzu just smiled and kept still. Eventually the others woke up too and from the general silence, Julius knew that they were feeling as awkward as he was.

'You may go now,' said Lao-tzu.

They bowed to him and left the room in silence. Once in the corridor Faith, Skye and Morgana joined Julius.

'I can't believe I fell asleep,' said Morgana dejectedly.

'We all did,' said Faith.

'Yeah, but I'm the one who's supposed to love hanging around in woods!' she cried.

'What was the point of that? Why didn't he wake us up?' asked Skye.

'Who knows? Mind you, I feel refreshed after that extended nap,' added Julius. 'But I really hope it's going to get better.'

They all nodded in agreement and headed off to the mess hall. The warmth of the garden was too enticing to ignore, so they took their lunch with them and sat on the grass.

Faith was eyeing his diary suspiciously. 'What am I supposed to write?' he said to no one in particular.

'Dear diary,' said Skye, 'I had my first Meditation class today. I slept for three hours. It was great!'

They all laughed at that and Julius felt that he could cope much better with his shameful performance, knowing that he wasn't alone.

After lunch they made their way back to the holographic sector for their Telekinesis class. A man was already there waiting for them. He was tall and imposing, with broad shoulders and thick legs. His face, devoid of any facial hair, was plump and red, as if a heart attack was never too far away. The corners of his blue eyes stretched into tiny smile-wrinkles, a sign of many hours spent in laughter, it seemed to Julius. With an inviting gesture, the man gathered the group around him and they bowed to each other.

'I am Professor Paul King,' he began with a booming voice. 'Telekinesis can be defined as movement from afar. It is the ability to manipulate objects mentally and, since you are standing in front of me, it is safe to assume that you all have that ability.'

Julius thought about his brother, Michael, and of the many times he had made him fly around the bedroom. At least this was something he was good at, so he wouldn't embarrass himself as he had done that morning.

'The possibilities of this particular White Art are endless, starting with your personal defence. Moreover, a highly trained mind can even pilot a spaceship remotely.'

'Now that's interesting,' thought Julius. He'd never known that something like that was actually possible.

'Obviously what makes this skill hard to manage is not so much *moving* the object, as *controlling* that movement. That will be your aim for this year, to perfect the ability to control.' As he said that, he uncovered a crate behind him. 'Take one of these objects and line up at the back wall, then place it at your feet.'

Julius grabbed the first thing he found, a cube made of soft material. When they were ready, King told them to make their objects slide across the floor to the other end of the room. Julius locked his eyes on his cube and felt a familiar click inside his head. Then he pushed. The cube crossed the floor in a straight line, without lifting from the ground. He looked around and was pleased to discover that he had been the first. Faith's cube was rolling over the floor and Morgana's was floating to its destination. Only Skye had it sliding along the surface, but not in a straight line.

King let them try it a few more times before splitting them into pairs. Julius was paired with Faith, and they were told to go to opposite sides of the room and face each other. They were then instructed to send the object back and forth between them. After several minutes however, Faith was still struggling to keep the cube from rolling and Julius was getting bored, so he started to pull Faith toward him along with the cube. At first Faith couldn't understand what was happening, but when he saw Julius laughing, he slammed his brakes on.

'I'd like to see you try that now, smarty. This baby's got hydraulic brakes!'

Obviously it was a tempting invitation and Julius obliged him. Not knowing what kind of resistance Faith's chair would pose, he pulled a little harder than normal and before he knew it he found himself pinned to the wall by Faith and his chair. They burst out laughing, quickly followed by the rest of the class, who had stopped to see what had happened.

'As you can see,' said King with a raised eyebrow, 'the possibilities are *indeed* endless.'

The rest of the lesson flew by and when they left, Julius and Faith started laughing again, thinking of how they would record the incident in their diaries.

On Tuesday morning, Julius awoke at eight, leaving plenty of time to wash and get dressed – he really wasn't a morning person. Feeling slightly more human, he joined his friends in the mess hall for a quick breakfast. Once finished, they headed off to their very first Draw lesson, still trying to figure out exactly what the "draw" in question was. Faith was convinced that they were supposed to paint using only their minds; Skye and Julius thought it was where they would learn how to draw up legal documents, in case they ended up working for the Curia; Morgana reckoned that it must be something to do with extracting information from people, using some undefined power. Their teacher, a wiry middle-aged woman with a remarkably long nose, by the name of Professor Cathy Turner, put them out of their misery a few minutes later, leaving them all dumbstruck.

'The power of drawing,' explained Turner, looking over her spectacles, 'is one of the most difficult White Arts to master. It allows the recipient to draw energy – life, if you like – from another living organism.' She paused for a moment, to let the words sink in more effectively. 'Using White Arts depletes energy. Should you find yourself in a combat situation, the presence of something as small as a flower could save your life. Marcus Tijara himself was the first to discover and study this art. Every person who has been affected by the Chemical War carries the genes that allow the draw, but as with every other art, and perhaps more so, drawing requires an incredible amount of control: should you use it untamed, on another human being, you could kill them.'

Professor Turner seemed satisfied with the look of horror on the students' faces and proceeded to distribute little cactus plants among them.

'Since you have just woken up and had breakfast, your energy levels are at their fullest. Therefore, you shall not be able to draw too much. Your cacti have flowers – if the draw is successful, one of the flowers should wither.' As she spoke, she placed a plant on her desk and stood over it while the students gathered around her. She cupped her hands around the plant, as if to shelter it from a wind. Julius watched her fingertips, which were moving slightly, as if feeling for something imperceptible. Suddenly she took a deep breath and held it for a few seconds. At that moment, several students pointed at the cactus, whispering. Julius watched, mouth open, as one of the pink flowers began to wither before falling onto the desk – she had sucked the life from it. After the demonstration, Professor Turner sent the students back to their desks. She then made her way around the class, trying to explain to each of them in turn how they were meant to accomplish the draw.

Julius saw that both Skye and Faith successfully withered their flowers a little. When Turner stopped at Julius's desk, he had recovered from his initial surprise, and since the others were busy writing down first impressions or trying the draw again, he felt ready enough to try.

'Now Mr McCoy, are you relaxed?' she asked him. Julius nodded and she continued. 'Every living organism is surrounded by an energy field. Your fingertips need to feel it. When you have found it, you have to concentrate and *pull* that energy into you. A sudden, deep inhalation is all that it takes to draw. I'm going to connect this energy receiver to your arm, to record how much you draw.'

She placed an electrode on his forearm and Julius tried to relax. He placed his hands around the plant, closed his eyes and started to feel for the energy. It took him a minute before he could feel anything, and when he did, he took a sudden, deep breath and held it. In his mind he could see a blue smoky fluid entering his fingertips, and spreading all the way up his arms to his shoulders, accompanied by a tingling sensation.

He slowly opened his eyes and looked at the plant. To his disappointment however, the flowers were all still attached and looking distinctly perky. The colours had possibly faded a little, but

63

that was all. He looked at Professor Turner, starting to apologise, but stopped in mid-sentence. She was staring, slack-jawed, at his energy receiver over the rim of her glasses. Julius looked at the little needle on the monitor and saw that it was stuck all the way up to the maximum. Somehow, he had charged it completely without killing the plant.

His teacher's hands were still firmly planted on the desk. Julius was trying to decide whether to say something, when he noticed that her digital watch had stopped. Right at that moment, Professor Turner shook herself from her reverie, hurriedly gave Julius a new energy receiver, shovelled three new pots of cacti onto his desk and gathered the old one up in her arms.

'Keep trying, class. I'll return shortly,' she said, rushing out of the room.

The other students turned curiously towards Julius, who shrugged his shoulders, not knowing himself what had happened.

Professor Turner returned twenty minutes later, and the lesson continued without further incident. When the bell rang, she dismissed them with a quick bow.

'Could someone close the door please,' she called to her students.

Julius was the last to leave and as he grabbed the handle to pull the door shut behind him, an electric discharge shot through his fingers. The door swung from his grasp, pushed by this jolt, slammed against the wall and banged shut an inch from his face. He stood there, dumbstruck until he heard Professor Turner's footsteps advancing menacingly towards the door.

'Who is the student who wants a detention so much, that he feels the need to slam my door?'

Julius didn't wait for her to find out, but turned on his heels and headed for the exit at a gallop. When he joined the others in the mess hall, Morgana asked about his draw.

'Even when Professor Turner came back, she was still rather distracted,' said Morgana over her soup. 'I mean, she actually put her hands on the spikes of the cactus during my demonstration. What did you do, Julius?'

'I'm not sure. I did draw some energy, but the flower stayed on.' It was true enough and, although the fact that Professor Turner's watch had stopped was still puzzling him, he really didn't understand what had happened and decided not to share that information with them.

'How much energy did you draw?' asked Faith.

'I maxed out the receiver,' muttered Julius.

'And the plant?'

'Nothing happened to it. No withering.'

They kept eating in silence for a while. Then Skye turned to Julius: 'You could check it out, you know? In the library I saw a chip about drawing. If Marcus Tijara was involved in it, he might have left some notes.'

Julius thought that sounded like a good idea, and decided to check it out sometime before the next Draw class.

That afternoon's much anticipated first Martial Arts lesson, turned out to be a major disappointment as Professor Lee Chan was out of school for the day on business. Instead they ended up in a Grey Art classroom studying anatomy of the human body, supervised by a very serious Nathan Cress.

Wednesday arrived and nobody, except Morgana, was looking forward to that morning's lesson. The Spaceology teacher, Lucy Brown, was an ageing woman with long white hair, who spoke excitedly about every facet of the stars and planets. The first lesson was about the Solar System, and as Professor Brown started to explain that the Sun contained about 99.9 per cent of the System's total mass, Julius's attention sunk by about that percentage. To pass the time, he started to move pens and rulers with his mind over to Faith and Skye, occasionally hitting a classmate along the way. Morgana was furiously taking notes, since this subject bore great relevance to her dream career as a spaceship pilot, and was throwing furious glances over to the boys every time an eraser hit her on the head.

Afterwards, during lunch, they were relieved to find out that Professor Lee Chan had returned, and so they changed into their tracksuits before entering the holographic sector.

The room had taken on the appearance of a dojo, with wooden floors and padded walls. Professor Chan could have been the lost twin brother of Len Lao-tzu – the only difference was that his clothes were all black and his goatee was still brown. When they were all kneeling on the floor, he began.

'I apologise for my absence yesterday, however, I understand you all had a chance to revise anatomy and knowing how our bodies work is fundamental to this discipline. We study this Grey Art for various reasons: fitness, mental discipline, self-defence and combat skills. Although there are many martial arts, the one that will concern us is the Mindkata. A kata is a set routine of techniques performed alone, or sometimes with a partner. The development of your mind-skills, or White Arts, as we call them, is a major part of your training. Therefore our katas are devised for their benefit. Miss Louisa Call,' he said to a small, red haired girl. 'Volunteer, if you please.'

Louisa walked forward, looking more than a little worried. Chan placed a wooden chair in front of her and then asked her to step back.

'If you were to remove an object from your path using telekinesis, what position would you assume?'

Louisa extended one arm forward, open palm facing the chair. Chan asked her to push the chair backwards and she did. It slid to the end of the room and bounced off the wall.

'Thank you, Miss Call. You may rejoin your classmates. How many of you assume that same position?' asked Chan.

Almost every student put their hand up.

'As a martial artist, you will learn a more effective technique for performing that action.' Chan pulled the chair back to its original position, with his mind. He stood with his legs slightly apart, left foot forward. Both his arms were bent by his sides, parallel with his feet. His left hand was bunched into a fist and, of his right hand, only the index and third finger were outstretched, the other two bent under the thumb. Quick as a cat, he shot both his right hand and foot forward simultaneously. As he did so, he let out a sharp breath, like a gust of wind, and in an instant the chair smashed against the back wall.

'Rapid!' said Faith, ecstatically.

'Quite so, Mr Shanigan,' said Chan, turning to face them. 'What did I just do, Mr McCoy?'

'You used your fingers as ... a channel?' answered Julius tentatively.

'Correct, although your entire body is a channel. The powers that you unleash outwards come from within, therefore you can freely choose what means you use to release them. Arms, fingers and legs, because of their shape, create a perfect channel for shooting energy. Next year, you will be introduced to the Gauntlet – it is a device worn on the back of your hand, an outlet for your energy. It gives a colour to it, allowing you to see and control its direction.'

'I wonder,' whispered Faith to Julius, 'can you use your nose as an outlet?'

'I thought your bum would do better!' answered Julius, trying hard not to laugh.

'I could turn me chair into a rocket!' The picture of Faith lifting off was enough to bring tears to both their eyes.

'Perhaps we should give that a try, Mr Shanigan,' Chan's voice suddenly thundered over their heads.

Julius and Faith tried hard to pull themselves together, but their teacher wasn't moved, and as punishment they ended up doing weights for one hour. That night, Julius was quite unable to walk. His entire body was aching and following a quick bite and a shower, he decided to call it a day. When he entered his room, Skye was sitting at his desk, writing. Julius nodded to him and slowly lowered himself onto his reclining chair.

'You don't look too shiny, mate,' said Skye putting down his pen.

'Never mind … what are you up to?'

'Oh, just writing home. If Mum doesn't hear from me regularly, she'll think I'm dead … or worse.'

Julius nodded and thought about the promise he had made to Michael. He couldn't have written to him that night anyway, given that he was unable to even lift his arms and that he had to drink his soup through a straw. So he made a mental note for the end of the week and collapsed exhausted on his bed.

That Friday morning, he and the rest of his classmates were lined up outside the holographic classroom by 08:30 sharp, for their first Pilot Training lesson. When their teacher arrived, Julius could see that he was clearly pleased.

'I have had eager students before, but thirty minutes early? It's a record!' he said with a smile, and ushered them inside the room.

The Professor introduced himself as Farid Clavel, a young man from Lebanon. His uniform was as tidy as was expected of all Zed officers, but Julius thought that his face had a pleasant, relaxed look to it.

The classroom had already been prepared, with thirty simulation cockpits all facing Professor Clavel in two semi-circles.

'Before we start,' said Clavel, 'there is someone I would like you to meet.' As he said that, an old black man with candid white hair stepped inside the room.

'This is Mr Pete Kingston from Mississippi, the owner of Pit-Stop Pete,' said Clavel.

Pete smiled at the class.

'Mr Kingston runs an outer docking base in our orbit. Ships come from all over to use his services – from refuelling, to repairs, to construction. No doubt someone in this class will choose to spend their summer camp doing work experience at Pete's'.

Julius could see that Faith was smiling at Pete unashamedly and knew already that his friend would put his tent up in that dock for the whole summer. Pete told them they were all welcome to visit him at any time and, before leaving, Julius watched as he whispered to Professor Clavel, throwing occasional glances at Faith. He found that odd, but perhaps it was just a coincidence.

The lesson finally started, and when Julius sat down in his cockpit, he was really excited. They spent the morning familiarising themselves with all the buttons, levers, panels and screens, over and over again. In the afternoon, Professor Clavel made them work in pairs, so they could question each other about what button did what, route-finding and how to set coordinates for a hyperjump, a facility that all Zed aircraft possessed.

Julius had thoroughly enjoyed the day, even when Faith tried to swap all the controls around because apparently he knew a way of making them more functional. By four o'clock, he knew how to start a spaceship without destroying the engines. As he sat in his room that night, Julius read over his diary entries again. Then he took his laptop and began to write to his brother, Michael, about all the excitement of his very first week at the Zed Academy.

A BIRTHDAY'S BEST GIFT

'I can't believe we've been here a month already,' said Julius one Friday at lunchtime.

He was lying under an oak tree in the garden with his mates, digesting a particularly heavy lunch. The school had become as familiar to him as his own home, and he had settled into the routine quite easily. Nothing ever seemed to change in Tijara, from the spring-like temperature to the sunny sky. Yet, he felt like he had done and learned more in the past month than in all of his 12 years on Earth.

The lessons *had* picked up pace, however, and the teachers had been giving them plenty of homework. Most evenings he could be found in the library doing research or in the holographic sector improving his Mindkata techniques and telepathic control. Professor Turner had made no further comments on his first draw, so he had put the whole cactus incident out of his mind. Besides, he was now able to draw some energy from the little flowers like most of his classmates.

In Meditation, Professor Lao-tzu had let him fall asleep for three weeks, before Julius could exhort himself to stay awake, even if no relaxation had been achieved as yet. Out of their class, only Morgana had managed to stay awake from the second week, but Julius wasn't surprised by that. For many years Morgana had forced him to walk with her in the Highlands, or to sit along the shore of Loch Lomond for hours on end, just soaking up the surroundings – she positively thrived on those sensations.

Morgana was sitting against the oak tree, staring at the stream and looking quite content. Julius knew why: her sister Kaori had just left, having shared lunch with them. She was two years older than Morgana but they were very much alike in both personality and looks. Julius had spent some time with Kaori back home, but as they grew up, the difference in age had become more prominent and she had found an older group of friends. On the subject of friends, Julius had found himself reflecting quite often about how lucky he had been to meet Faith and Skye. They were quite different from each other, Faith with his quirkiness and Skye with his natural enthusiasm, but they were both honest, straightforward people, which Julius appreciated a lot.

Lost in these thoughts, he suddenly remembered that the day after tomorrow would be Faith's birthday. He would have to speak with Morgana and Skye to organise him a present, and quickly. Turning towards Morgana, he called her with his mind. She flinched a little, startled.

'*I need to talk to you,*' he thought.

'*What's up?*' she thought back, still looking at the stream.

'*It's Faith's birthday on Sunday and, maybe if you take him away for a little while, I can organise something with Skye.*'

'*Sure. I'll get him over to the holographic sector or something. Can you let me hear what you say to Skye?*'

'*Hey, I'm not a conference network facility you know!*'

'*All right, but let me know what you decide.*'

'*Sure. Thanks a lot.*'

Morgana stood up and, with the excuse of revising flight techniques before that afternoon's pilot lesson, she managed to lure Faith away. As they were leaving, Julius noticed that Skye was about to stand up as well, so he quickly sent him a mind message: '*Don't move. And don't say anything!*'

Skye couldn't have moved even if had wanted to. He had never received a mind message from Julius before and so sat where he was, petrified.

Once the other two had disappeared, Julius turned to him: 'Sorry. I didn't mean to scare you.'

'That was freaky. For a moment I thought my father was behind me.'

Julius explained the situation to him quickly, aware that they only had a few minutes left of their lunchtime.

'How many Fyvers do we have?' asked Skye.

'I managed to get 30 for September. But we can only go to Satras in two weeks' time.'

'Hey, why don't we give some Fyvers to Kaori? I'm sure she can get us something before Sunday.'

'That's a good idea. I'll give Morgana a tenner tonight then, with a list of possible presents. She can get them to Kaori.'

With the present organised, they headed off to class. The first thing they noticed when they entered was that their cockpits had been replaced with individual desks. When Julius sat down, he saw that the surface of the desk was in fact a touch screen.

Farid Clavel waited for them all to be seated before beginning the lesson. 'As you know, all weapons have been banned since the

Chemical War. Because over half of the population was decimated during that period, the Earth Leader, together with the five Voices of Earth, representing each continent, successfully implemented the ban. Only the White and Grey Arts were allowed to be used as protection for the human race. In Space, we have not been involved in a large scale conflict since the Arneshians' attack on Zed, back in Marcus Tijara's time. However, one of the purposes of Zed is that we be ready, should that threat, or any other, arise again.'

Julius watched Clavel closely. Since the rumours of a possible conflict between Zed and the Arneshians had begun that April, he had not heard any further news. Clavel's face, however, was unusually serious while he discussed the topic, and it occurred to Julius that perhaps the Space Channel had not been too far off in its predictions.

'If you look at your screen, you will see that I have uploaded some schematics for you,' continued Clavel. 'Spaceship combat is possible because of this device, the ship catalyst. Professor Chan has mentioned the Gauntlet to you – this device is its equivalent. A ship can have as many catalysts as is needed but it is important to remember that a person is required to operate each one. The device channels your energies and amplifies them as much as required.'

Just then Professor Chan entered the classroom and, after a short exchange with Clavel, with several glances thrown in the direction of Faith, he turned to the class: 'Mr Shanigan, please follow me.'

Julius saw that Morgana was looking at him, puzzled, but he could only shrug his shoulders in reply, feeling as clueless as she was. Faith hovered over to Chan and followed him out of the room. Julius could have sworn that there was a look of anxiety on his face. He remembered that there had been a similar exchange between Pit-

Stop Pete and Clavel, during their first week in Tijara, and he hoped Faith wasn't in any kind of trouble. In fact, he was so preoccupied that by the time the lesson ended he had very little recollection of what they had been shown.

By nine o'clock that night, however, they were all worried because Faith had still not returned. Resolved to find out what was going on, Julius, Morgana and Skye started along the corridor towards the teachers' offices, in search of someone who could help them. As they were approaching the main gate, Professor Chan crossed their path.

'Professor,' said Julius with a quick bow, 'could you tell us where Faith Shanigan is?'

'Mr Shanigan will spend tonight in the infirmary room.'

'Is he all right?' asked Morgana, clearly flustered.

'He is quite well, Miss Ruthier. He only needs to … get used to his new situation,' said Chan with a smile. 'You can visit him in the morning though.'

With that, he bowed and walked away, leaving them even more puzzled than before. They waited for him to disappear into the staff dorms, and then ran to the infirmary sector, only to find it shut.

'Julius, can't you send him one of your freaky mind messages?' asked Skye, trying to force the door open.

'I was trying but I can't get through,' answered Julius, shouldering the door.

'Boys, leave that door standing, please,' said Morgana looking behind her. 'If Foster catches us, he'll probably throw us out of an airlock or something.' The Head of Security's name was scary enough to make them stop, and so they decided to leave.

'At least we know he's fine,' said Julius, but that night he couldn't stop wondering about Faith's "new situation".

At eight o'clock the following morning, Julius and Skye picked up Morgana and made their way to the infirmary. As they entered, an incredible sight greeted them – Faith was gliding towards them in an upright position.

'Guys,' he cried ecstatically, 'check out me birthday present. It's rapid!'

Julius stopped in his tracks, eyes wide open. Faith was wearing what looked like a long, conical shaped skirt. It was blue like their uniforms and seemed to be made out of horizontal panels, slightly overlapping each other. They couldn't see his feet, just a small gap between the bottom of the skirt and the floor.

'Well that's a new situation and no mistakes,' said Julius, grinning.

Faith explained to them how the school had ordered this new prototype for him, from Pit-Stop Pete. Professor Chan had spent the afternoon teaching him how to use it and Dr Dritan Walliser, the resident physician, had inserted a number of sensors into his legs. Since that last piece of news had made his friends drop their jaws, Faith decided to show them exactly what he meant.

'See, the skirt-frame is fixed to me waist like a belt, and harnessed underneath. The bottom of the frame has the same devices as me old chair: I can hover or glide, or use the emergency wheels – just in case – and if I have to sit down,' he said, gliding towards a bench, 'me brain interacts with the magnetic field of the frame which will make me legs bend accordingly, by activating the corresponding sensors.' He bent forward slightly and, as he did so, the bottom panels began to slide upwards, the lower ones under the ones above them. When they reached Faith's knees, they stopped. He was still hovering, but then his knees started to bend and the frame landed him gently on the seat.

Julius had been speechless throughout this demonstration while Morgana, holding her hands to her chest, had a little tear rolling down her cheek.

'Oh Faith,' was all she managed to say.

Faith noticed her reaction and turned vaguely to Julius and Skye, slightly red in the face.

'This is just!' said Julius. 'Come on, we're going to show you off.'

They left the infirmary and went straight to the mess hall. Needless to say, Faith and his "skirt" became the centre of attention for the whole weekend. They couldn't walk anywhere without being stopped by groups of students asking for a demonstration. Faith happily obliged them each time, and by Sunday night his control of the frame was as smooth as could be. In light of this development, Julius had agreed with the others to postpone buying the birthday present until they went to Satras themselves, so that Faith could choose some new gadget for his skirt. On Sunday night, they gave Faith a card instead and promised to take him shopping soon.

As their first visit to Satras was approaching, the Hologram Palace was all the 1 Mizki Juniors could talk about. Every meal time would see the first year students huddled in groups, discussing the latest scores and arguing about who was the best of the best. One Friday evening, Julius was having a snack in the garden with Skye and two other students from their year, Gustavo Perez and Yuri Slovich, both from the colonies. Perez had gathered information about the games from an older student and was sharing his knowledge enthusiastically.

'You can compete in different formats, but the ultimate glory comes from playing Solo, and being good at it. Or else you can play regular games as a team – it can be as large or as small as you like. It can represent a year, a nation, or even a continent. Or it can be just you and your roommate if you like.'

'Obviously only teams from the same category can compete against each other,' added Yuri. 'So, for example, you and Skye couldn't compete against a national team.'

'Yes we could,' cried Skye, 'and we would kick ...'

'Yeah, yeah,' cut in Yuri. 'Wait until you start before you boast. There's nasty competition out there.'

'Like who?' asked Julius.

'See that guy over by the stream?' said Yuri, pointing over his shoulder.

'What, the one surrounded by girls?' said Skye in awe.

'The very one: Bernard Docherty, a 5 Mizki Senior. He's the Solo Champion for the whole of Zed. Only the top ten high scores are displayed for the Solo game – the first is his, the other nine have been there for the last fifty years.'

Julius watched as Docherty sat on a bench, his long legs stretched out before him. A small crowd was gathered around him. He must have been talking about something exceptionally interesting, judging by the look of admiration from the boys, and by the adoring glances of the girls.

'What are the team games like?' asked Julius, still looking at Docherty.

'The main difference,' Gustavo answered, 'is that in team games you use your Grey Arts, like piloting or martial arts, whereas in Solo it's all about your White Skills and how strong your mind powers are. There are different kinds of group games. Broadly speaking, you can divide them into two categories: combat simulation and flight, which are racing games. But, even if you should race fifty times in a row, the tracks always change – the computer randomises it that way.'

'That's another way that Solo games are different,' added Yuri. 'They can be race, fight, or a bit of both, only you don't get to decide. But, whatever comes up when you enter the simulator, the difficulty level remains the same.' He glanced at his watch and said, 'Anyway guys, we need to go. And Skye, my mum says that your mum wants you to write to her, or she'll chuck all of your surfboards into a black hole.'

'Right, thanks Yuri,' said Skye, looking distressed.

'What's it like on the colonies?' asked Julius, after Yuri and Gustavo had left.

Skye propped himself up on his elbows and plucked the grass blades around his hands. 'Weird,' he said, smiling at Julius. 'People think that, just because we're far away from the Curia and Earth, we sing and dance all day.'

'Don't you?' asked Julius, teasingly.

'Maybe on the *actual* colonies they do, but not where I come from. My home is on Terra 3, one of the Zed space stations in the Indus constellation.'

'I thought that all space settlements belonged to Earth,' said Julius, a little confused.

'The colonies do, but they were formed after the three Zed space stations were built. Only an active member of Zed, graduated from the schools, can live on them. My dad for example, studied at Tuala and now works on Terra 3. When he married, my mum moved there too, and when he retires they have to move back to Earth, or to one of the colonies.'

'What if you have a brother who doesn't get selected for the Academy?'

'Then, when he's sixteen, he has to move out and start a life for himself.'

'Can you find work in these places?'

'Sure. There's always something needing done when humans are around – you can open a hairdresser's if you really want! Obviously you can't live in a villa surrounded by trees, but if you fancy a day in the country you just use the holodeck.'

'Being out there,' said Julius, creasing his eyebrows, 'weren't you ever afraid of being attacked by the Arneshians?'

'I thought about it sometimes. But Dad said they wouldn't dare. The space stations are well protected and, besides, the Arneshians would have to pass by Zed before reaching us. *And* they don't have any mind-skills.'

'None?' asked Julius.

'Don't they teach you space history on Earth?' asked Skye.

'I would have studied that in high school, if I hadn't been selected for Zed. As it is, I haven't had a chance yet. Wanna bring me up to scratch, oh smart one?'

'For you? Sure,' said Skye, flashing him a wink and sitting up. 'Lesson one: Clodagh Arnesh – she was Marcus Tijara's friend and colleague. They researched the mind-skills together – only Arnesh didn't have any. Instead, she was incredibly gifted at everything technological, which was also a knock-on effect of the Chemical War. When they opened the Zed Academy, Arnesh established the Grey Arts and taught them in this very school. She invented Mindkata and was one hell of an engineer. Faith would have loved her. Then fame went to her head and she desired to become the Earth Leader, since she had done so much for it with her studies. But, with no mind-skills, she needed Marcus's support. She tried to convince him to join her in her power quest, but Marcus refused. Arnesh was envious of his talents, and so were her supporters: all folks with no mind-skills, just like her. They fought, until Marcus banished Clodagh and her followers to the Taurus constellation. She settled on a planet in the Pleiades star cluster and named it Arnesh. A few years later, Marcus created some sort of powerful weapon to use as a defence in case Arnesh decided to return, which she did. Marcus's weapon did work, however both he and Clodagh were killed. Nobody really knows how or why, although my dad believes that someone does know, but they just won't tell us. Some of her followers survived obviously, and they retreated to Arnesh to bide their time.'

'So, even if they were banished, they could still come back?' asked Julius.

'Of course. Since Clodagh's death, there's always been a ruler on Arnesh who has tried to complete her quest – now they have Queen Salgoria, a direct descendant of Clodagh Arnesh, who's been walking in her great-great-great-grandmother's footsteps. Heck, we've even had our fair share of kidnappings in Satras.'

'What?' said Julius, taken aback.

'Well, at least it's thought that it was the Arneshians, although it can't be proved. The last person disappeared four years ago. He was Tuala's Master at the time, Bastiaan Grant. That one really shook things up in the Curia and they tried hard to cover it up with the Space Channel.'

'Did they ever find him?'

'Kinda. He was dead.'

'But why would the Arneshians kidnap folks?'

'Who knows. Although, I remember one of my dad's conversations back home, after they found Grant. He was talking about some kind of experiments that had been done on his body. Anyway, don't worry about it – our borders are well guarded by the fleet. If they did try to re-enter, we would know.'

A sudden shiver ran down Julius's back. He didn't feel like sitting outside anymore. The black sky seemed quite ominous to him after their conversation and he wanted to be back within the safety of the school's walls. Later that night, as he was tossing and turning in his bed, he struggled to shake the feeling that the Arneshians could in fact re-enter their galaxy somehow. If the Space Channel reports were anything to go by, it could already have happened.

SATRAS

One Saturday morning, Julius and one hundred other students gathered at the train stop outside Tijara's gates. The crowd was so excited that, when the train arrived, Julius was almost lifted off the floor and had to elbow his way into the compartment. By the next stop, when another 100 students boarded from the Tuala School stop, they were all jammed in like sardines in a tin. The train finally stopped at the Satras platform, which lay at the opening of a large cave situated at the centre of a gentle ridge. Julius wedged his way out of the carriage with some difficulty, only to find himself piled against a mass of bodies in the queue for the security checkpoint. Together with Skye he tried to protect Faith from getting squashed, skirt and all, while Morgana and Siena, a pretty Italian brunette in their year, pushed forward through the crowd ahead of them to create some space. When they finally reached the entrance, they had to separate and walk single file through a set of turnstiles, as if they were entering a football stadium, only instead of handing over their tickets they had to look into a retinal scanner.

When they finally emerged on the other side, they found themselves standing on a large terrace overlooking Satras. Julius gasped in wonder, as it was more amazing than he had ever imagined. The town itself was carved into the rocky mantle of the Moon, rather than above the surface, and its look reminded him of the inside of the *Colosseo* of Rome. Someone had excavated tunnels and caves all around, now occupied by shops, cafes, restaurants and hotels, all covered in neon lights. Thin bridges criss-crossed in mid-air, linking all the facilities. They were packed with students running from one level to the other. Streams of emerald green water flowed out from hollows, cascading over the rocks and crashing with a roar into a large central lake. All around its shores were small tables with benches, where visitors could sit and enjoy the view of the waterfalls and the little wooden boats floating peacefully on the surface of the pool below. It was always night in Satras but, with the neon lights and the emerald water, the whole town glowed like an eerie light bulb.

The town had been built at the same time as the Curia and the schools. It was a place that served numerous functions: the ministers would meet there to conduct business, to welcome delegations from the colonies and to hold official receptions. As only Zed members were allowed inside the schools or the Curia, all visitors would converge here, where they could be accommodated in one of the many hotels. The students would come to spend their hard earned Fyvers in the various shops and cafes of Satras, but mainly in the famous Hologram Palace. There were also rumours of unofficial, secretive business transactions being conducted once all the students had returned to their respective schools, although no employee would ever have admitted to that.

'Look there – on the other side!' cried Julius.

Opposite the terrace and across the lake was a tall tower protruding out of the Moon's jagged rocks and stretching all the way to the ceiling. Above the entry archway, the words "Hologram Palace" were carved into the rocky face.

'Let's get down there. Come on!' said Skye, running towards the platform-lifts at the side of the terrace.

There were six lifts in total, continuously moving in a loop from the entrance to the ground floor. A man stood by the lifts, helping people step carefully over the gap. Julius was suddenly reminded of the ferris wheel back home, which was mounted every year in Princes Street gardens for the Hogmanay celebrations. Together with Michael, he would pester his dad to take them there with the repeated and often broken promise that they would not use their skills to make the wheel go faster.

Julius and Skye stepped lightly onto the lift, Skye giving his hand to Morgana in a proper, gentlemanly manner, while Faith smoothly hovered his way over.

'You know,' said Julius, eyeing Faith's skirt, 'if this thing crashes you'd be the only one left alive, with that gliding gadget of yours.'

'I hope not – you still owe me a birthday present!'

'Oh, really?' said Skye. 'How would you like a pink ribbon to go with your bloomers?'

That made them laugh so much that the lift shook beneath their feet. Several of their fellow passengers shot frightened stares at them as a result, so they quickly calmed down.

'We'll look for your present later,' said Julius to Faith. 'Let's go shake that tower up first.'

Once on the ground, they stepped off the lift and pushed their way through the crowd, oblivious to all the bustling around them. Reaching the gate of the Palace, Julius stopped and looked up. The tower was so tall that he couldn't see its top, his view further hindered by the green reflections thrown up by the water. They walked through the Palace gate and into a well lit hall. Small monitors were fitted all along its walls so that visitors could check the availability of the rooms and sign up for games. There was also a smaller section of screens where rooms could be booked for other functions, such as entertaining guests, worshipping or simply relaxing. In the centre of the hall was a kiosk, manned by an extremely wrinkled old lady. Her name badge identified her as Mrs Mayflower. Above her head, a sign read "Information and bookings". Three arches yawned out behind the kiosk – signposts indicated that the side ones led to the hologram rooms and the central one to the arena.

They walked through the middle arch into the inner ring, which was cluttered with small groups of students. Some of them were debating what to play and who should play what; others were just sitting on the large steps, watching the games unfold on the giant screens surrounding the arena.

'I think we should go for a racing game,' said Skye after a few minutes.

'Excellent idea!' said Morgana excitedly. 'I feel like showing off a little.'

'I'm in,' said Julius. 'What about the teams? Two against two, or …'

Julius broke off as Billy Somers barged his way through the crowd, followed by three other Sield students.

'I think you should race against *us*,' he said to Julius, with a smirk. 'And we'll play with a girl too, to make up for the guy in the skirt.'

Julius didn't reply but instead looked at Faith with an "Are you going to let him get away with that?" expression on his face. Faith smiled in his usual unconcerned fashion and gestured for Somers to lead the way.

As the Sield students walked past them, the girl turned to Faith and stopped. 'I can't really stand his big mouth,' she said in a light French accent, pointing at Somers. 'I only want to play. I'm Amelie by ze way, and zey are Ben Clatt and Eric 'offson.'

Faith was clearly pleased by that remark of support and immediately introduced her to Julius and the others. Together they walked to the kiosk, where Somers had already booked a game.

'The game's a race,' said Somers. 'Two teams, eight planes. Last pilot standing wins. Let's go!' Somers started towards the left door, calling his team to him with an arrogant snap of his fingers.

Julius's eyes widened in disbelief. 'Did you see that?'

'How anyone can stand that pompous bore is beyond my comprehension,' added Morgana with a shake of her head.

Somers's team mates weren't impressed either.

'Does he think we're his dogs or something?' said Eric.

'This is the first and last time I play with him,' answered Ben, snapping his fingers back in the direction of Somers.

Julius was standing just behind them and listened to their outraged comments with delight.

Beyond the left door, a set of stairs led them downward until the corridor split into two paths. Julius saw that the one on the left was signed "Combat" and the other "Flight". They followed the right corridor, which led into a spacious room where several other 1 Mizki Juniors were already gathered.

'If I can have your attention please,' a male voice cried over the group. 'My name is Mr Smith, the Flight sector technician. As this is your first time in the Hologram Palace, you need to listen up. Every time you play in teams you will come to this floor. Behind me are two changing rooms – girls to the right – where you will be given your holosuit. Get changed and wait inside until your team is called. Leave through the green portal and a technician will lead you to your individual holosphere. During flight games, you will pilot a one-man vessel through a series of obstacles. This plane is built exactly like a Cougar, which is Zed's fastest aircraft.'

Morgana tugged excitedly at Julius's sleeve when she heard that, while he actively ignored her and continued listening to Mr Smith's instruction.

'To remove the obstacles and the enemies out of your path, you will use only the plane's laser gun. Now, to remove an enemy Cougar from the game, first you have to shoot them – if you hit them in the right spot, a circle will appear above the plane; second, you have to fly your plane through your enemy's circle. When you've accomplished both of those tasks, they will disappear from the game. Your own mind-skills will be blocked off and cannot be used during team games. If you want to show off, you'll have to play Solo. Now, get changed!'

The buzz of excitement accompanying that last order was tangible. The technician watched the students entering their changing rooms and, as Julius's group approached the door, he called Faith to one side. 'When you've collected your holosuit, keep walking to the end of the room. There's a space there where you can get changed more comfortably.'

Faith nodded and glided inside. Julius was pleased to hear that, since he really didn't want to see a repeat of what had happened in the changing rooms at the Zed Test Centre back in August.

The holosuit desk was near the door and Julius awaited his turn eagerly. When he reached the desk, the technician measured him with a critical eye and selected a holosuit from under the counter.

Grabbing it, he walked inside. The changing room was long, with lockers along both walls and metal benches running down its centre. The front of each locker had a small screen fixed to it. Opposite the entrance, were two doors to either side of the green portal. The one to the left must have led to shower rooms, thought Julius, judging by the cloud of steam puffing out of the door; the other one was the area where Faith had been directed to get changed.

'This looks just like my wetsuit,' said Skye, 'Only funkier!'

Julius examined his own holosuit – it was black, with bright blue sensors covering almost every inch of it, feet included, all the way up to the neck. He had never surfed in his life, so he copied Skye as he changed, trying not to look too clumsy as he did so.

'It's easier if you sit down,' said Skye. 'Start from your feet and work your way up, like when girls put tights on.

'How do *you* know how girls put their tights on?' asked Julius with a raised eyebrow.

Skye turned slightly red and with a wave of his hand said, 'Never mind that. It's a long story. Anyway, once around the waist put your arms in the sleeves. Zip is at the back.'

Julius followed the instructions quickly and then pulled the zip as far as he could. He felt a piece of cord hanging from its end, so with his other hand he grabbed hold of it from over his shoulder and pulled it up the rest of the way.

'You're a natural,' said Skye. 'You should come surfing with us sometime.'

'Maybe I will. By the way, we didn't really give a team name at the desk, did we?'

'I think Somers might have done it for us,' said Skye, looking slightly worried.

And sure enough, a few minutes later the loudspeaker called out the teams. 'Somers's Gang and the Skirts, make your way through the green portal.'

Keeping their heads very low, embarrassed as they were by their wonderful team name, Julius and Skye followed Somers toward the exit, muttering various unkind remarks behind his back. At the sight of the vast area that stretched out beyond the portal, however, all other thoughts left Julius's mind in a flash.

Contained within the vast area beyond were dozens of long rows of machines reaching to the other side of the room. These were obviously the holospheres that Morgana had told him about. The light was quite dim, but he thought that this floor could easily contain at least 300 players.

Morgana and Amelie emerged from their dressing rooms just in time, as a technician was calling their teams over to the left hand side of the floor. Julius followed them.

The metallic base of each holosphere was fixed to the floor with large bolts. Hovering above its base, a metal ring was glowing pale blue – it was inside this structure that the player had to go. Julius saw the technician lifting Faith off the floor and swiftly hoisting him up inside the ring. Faith grabbed two handles to either side of his head and raised himself up while the technician secured him quickly in place with a waist harness that was in turn attached to the ring. Next, he pressed a button on the back of the skirt and its panels retracted upwards, creating a thick belt around Faith's waist. The man then pushed a button on a remote control, activating the holosphere. Instantly, a magnetic field enveloped Faith, creating a shimmering bubble.

'You lot take the next seven,' said the man to the rest of the group.

Julius went for the holosphere next to Faith's, winking at him as he walked past. He lifted himself up using the handles and placed his feet onto two platforms. When everyone was ready, the technician activated all the spheres at once and all sound disappeared. Julius felt something tightening around his hands, waist and feet, but couldn't actually see any straps. Then a headrest slid down behind him. The pale blue field began to shake madly, sending ripples downward, and as the light became increasingly brighter Julius had to close his eyes tightly. Suddenly he felt as if his body had become weightless and he was no longer secured to the inner ring of the sphere. He opened one eye cautiously, just in time to see himself being lowered delicately inside his Cougar, which was just large enough to contain a comfortable leather seat and a small control panel. He sat there, mesmerised by the vast number of stars glittering in the infinite, dark expanse in front of him. During pilot training with Professor Clavel, they had never done a proper flight simulation in a hologram room. Usually, all that Julius could see from his training station was his classmates. Today for the first time, however, he would be experiencing what it was like to be a pilot on a real plane, and so far it felt great.

A red, intermittent light appeared in the darkness of the aircraft. Julius pushed it and all the controls came to life, illuminating the navigation helm.

'Julius, can you hear me?' Morgana's voice resounded in the aircraft.

'Loud and clear. Skye?'

'Yep. Faith?'

'Does Somers smell like a wet baboon?'

There was a brief snigger across the line.

'That would be a yes then. Morgana,' continued Julius, 'since you're the only one who's been here before, can you tell us what bit of the enemy's ship you have to hit to get the target circle to appear?'

'Actually, no. The sensor changes in every game, so you have to keep firing till you find it. It's half the fun. And mind the obstacles … they tend to be quite vicious. Use them as shields if you can, but shoot whatever you need to.'

'If I get hit,' said Faith 'take out Somers for me, will ya guys?'

There was no doubt that Julius would give it his all. He knew that it was just a game, nonetheless he still felt quite nervous. Suddenly a robotic voice echoed in his ear, counting down from five. Julius grabbed the handles of the u-shaped steering mechanism and took a deep breath. As the voice reached zero, he felt a mighty acceleration rush through the aircraft and he was shoved against his seat. He began to steady the Cougar into a straight line. There was no clear path that he could see, but his aircraft seemed to know exactly where to go, following some sort of spiralling, hyperactive rollercoaster track. As Julius couldn't see any obstacles coming his way, he started to practice some basic navigation movements. The controls were incredibly sensitive and the response was immediate.

'Julius, is that you driving like a drunken loony?' asked Faith.

'Sorry, I was just getting used to the system,' apologised Julius, steering away from Faith's aircraft.

'Hey!' cried Skye. 'I can see you both. I'm right below you. This is flashy!'

'When you're done fooling around,' said Morgana seriously, 'how about we go wipe them out?'

'Is she always this aggressive?' asked Skye, a hint of concern in his voice.

'Only when she's driving,' whispered back Julius.

'I heard that,' said Morgana speeding past them and disappearing from view in a downward spiral.

'Let's get them!' cried Skye, accelerating after her.

Julius let Faith fly ahead and then followed closely behind. Now that he was getting used to the navigation system, he had completely forgotten about being nervous. He looked over his shoulder through the glass hatch, which extended all the way to the tail of the Cougar, but there was no trace of Somers's group.

'Watch out!' said Morgana.

Julius looked up. Approaching fast, a group of meteorites was blocking the path. He saw Morgana's aircraft smoothly slipping through them and disappearing on the other side. He decided to follow her and accelerated towards a lower section, where the rocks were thinner. He tilted to one side and dived. Suddenly, a bright light flashed to his left and a delighted laugh echoed all around him.

'Did you see that?' cried Skye. 'I blasted my way through!'

Julius pulled level with Skye and gave him the thumbs up. He then accelerated forward to tail Morgana again.

It wasn't long before the next obstacle appeared in front of them. It looked like a giant windmill and it was blocking the entire track. Julius tried to judge the speed at which the blades were rotating, but that wasn't easy given that he was accelerating towards them at such a swift pace.

'Here goes nothing,' he said and dived straight between two blades as a gap appeared in front of him. He was sure his aircraft had scraped something, but he had made it through and his controls still seemed to be working fine. He could feel sweat on his face now and had to wipe it from his eyes with the back of his hand.

'Tornado right ahead!' cried Morgana. 'It'll swing you forward. Don't fight it.'

At the sight of the huge tower of swirling grey clouds, Julius automatically reduced his speed. Unperturbed, Faith whizzed past him and straight into the vortex.

'I'm through!' cried Faith excitedly a few seconds later.

Julius accelerated again and entered the grey column. He felt himself being pushed against the left hand side of his seat as the Cougar was treated to a full spin in the tornado. Then he was propelled forward and shot out like a stone from a sling. He steadied his aircraft as best he could, readying himself for the next surprise.

'Oh boy,' said Skye in a quivering voice. 'I think my breakfast is coming back up …'

'Breathe deeply,' said Julius, 'and do it quickly. I can see the next set.'

A large metal plate was blocking the entire track and the only way past it appeared to be through one of the many openings on its surface. Julius picked the uppermost one, but once inside he realised that it wasn't just a hole, but the beginning of a transparent pipe, twisting itself over and above the others. He couldn't steer more than a fraction to either side, which was probably a good thing since the track was really showing him the meaning of "evil rollercoaster". Suddenly, inside a pipe running level with his, he noticed another aircraft which Amelie was piloting. Julius felt a rush of adrenaline as he realised she had not yet spotted him. He slowed down just enough to let her fly ahead and ensure that her aircraft would come out first. After a few more seconds of inverted loops and sharp bends taken at furious speeds, Julius saw the end of his pipe. As he shot out of it, Amelie's Cougar was still ahead, to his right. He pulled up behind her and opened fire. Her aircraft swerved abruptly in panicked surprise. She started to fly unsteadily, but Julius kept on her tail and didn't stop firing. There were no visible objects ahead that she could use to shield herself and a few seconds later a bright yellow circle appeared above her aircraft.

'Don't lose her now,' Julius said to himself. He wasn't sure how long the target would remain active, so he quickly flew above her and lunged forward through the circle.

'Enemy destroyed,' said the robotic voice flatly.

'Hey, what happened?' said Morgana. 'Who did what to whom?'

'I got Amelie!' cried Julius ecstatically.

'Well done mate,' said Faith. 'One down and three to go!'

'Yes Julius, well d … oh damn!' cried Skye.

'What's the matter?' asked Julius, alarmed.

'It's Somers. He's right behind me!'

'Where are you? I can't see you.'

'I've just come out of the pipes of doom. He's firing like a maniac!'

'Hold on Skye!' said Faith. 'I can see you. Speed up!'

Julius slowed, wanting to give them some back up, but just then the next obstacle loomed into view. It was a giant humanoid robot, standing in the middle of the track and firing quick laser bursts from its eyes. Julius swerved all the way to the right, but the robot kept firing at him. He saw that the gap between its legs was the easiest way to pass him, so he banked sharply towards the centre of the track. Putting his aircraft into a horizontal spin to avoid getting hit, he shot through its leg without so much as a scratch. He was aware that the boys were still trying to shake Somers off, but they were well behind him now.

'Morgana, where are you?' said Julius.

'I've done a fast lap. There's one more obstacle after the robot. I've opened a path through it: bottom right corner. Hey, I can see Eric!'

'Go get him, girl.'

'Roger that!'

Julius kept looking back over his shoulder for Faith and Skye with no joy. The tension was mounting quickly. Then he heard Faith's voice coming through over the line: 'Skye, your target is up. Bend right!'

'I'm trying!' answered Skye. 'Oh bug ...'

'Allied destroyed,' said the now familiar robot-voice.

'Faith?' called Julius.

'Skye's gone, but I'm all over Somers like a rash!'

Julius was incredibly frustrated at not being able to see what was happening.

'I got his target up!' cried Faith. 'You are so mine, Somers.'

'Get him, Faith!' shouted Julius.

'I'm almost in ... almost ... almost ... Gotcha!'

'Enemy destroyed.'

Julius joined Faith in a bout of celebratory whooping.

'Enemy destroyed,' droned the voice once more.

'Sorry, that was me,' said Morgana cheerily. 'Eric is no more.'

'All hail the skirts of the team,' laughed Faith.

Julius was approaching the last obstacle now – a solid wall of overlapping plates. He saw the gap that Morgana had made and, with a big grin on his face, he flew straight in. Little did he know that Ben Clatt's aircraft was waiting in the darkness on the other side. At first Julius saw only a shadow to his left. It was only once he had returned to the middle of the track that Ben opened fire on him. His heart skipped a beat in surprise. Looking over his shoulder, he saw Ben's Cougar right on his tail.

'Get off me!' cried Julius, trying to shake him off.

He dived as fast as he could, then steered his Cougar into several twists and spirals, but Clatt was never too far behind. The first obstacle was approaching again and Julius noticed that many of the meteorites had disappeared from the bank, so he flew straight through a large central gap and kept accelerating. True to his memory, the windmill appeared soon afterwards. He opened fire against its blades and managed to blast open a safe passage without slowing down. As soon as he made it to the other side a red alert sound echoed inside his aircraft.

'Target activated,' said the voice flatly.

Julius maintained his breakneck speed, but Clatt's laser fire was all around him. Sweat poured down his face as he made a desperate sprint towards the tornado.

'Come on!' he told himself as the swirling column loomed closer.

For one brief moment, Julius really believed he would make it to the other side, but it was just then that Ben's aircraft flew straight through his target. Everything went dark and he felt as if a massive weight had entered his body, dragging him down into the seat. He opened his eyes and found himself back inside his holosphere. The technician walked over to him and deactivated his restraints.

'Game over, I'm afraid,' he said, helping Julius down. 'Make your way to the changing room so you can watch the end of the game.'

Julius nodded and headed for the exit, trying to keep his legs steady. He walked past Faith's holosphere and thought that he looked like someone in a deep sleep, but with a very agitated dream going on inside his head.

'Julius, come here quick!' called Skye from a corner of the changing room.

He was standing there with the upper part of his holosuit hanging around his waist, intently watching the screen on his locker with Eric.

'That was some chase man,' he said to Julius.

'Don't tell me. I must have sweated a couple of buckets.'

'Not as much as Clatt is sweating right now. Faith and Morgana are all over him. He doesn't stand a chance.'

Julius watched as the three aircrafts sped beneath the giant robot, trying to avoid being hit by its lasers. Once past it, Ben ended up between Faith, who was firing mercilessly from the left hand side, and Morgana, firing from the right. A few seconds later Clatt's yellow target appeared and Faith flew out in front of him, forcing him to pull back. As he did, Morgana, who was poised behind him, flew through the target and Ben's aircraft disappeared from view.

A line of writing scrolled across the screen: "The Skirts have won the game". Julius and Skye celebrated with a low five and shook hands with Eric. Somers, predictably, had already skulked off towards the showers.

Half an hour later Julius, Faith and Skye were sitting on the steps of the arena waiting for Morgana and, when she arrived, she ran to them with the biggest of smiles.

'That was some flying, lady,' said Faith, nodding in admiration.

'Yeah. I bet you'll become the best pilot in our year,' added Skye.

Morgana blushed slightly and gave a little bow.

'Well, I don't know about that, but we can definitely be the best team in our year!'

'As soon as we learn how not to get shot!' said Julius, looking towards Skye and laughing.

'Come on, you guys were great too,' answered Morgana. 'Besides, Julius, you're in the charts for first kill.'

'That will save my honour, this time at least.'

They left the Hologram Palace, still talking about their race, and Julius was surprised to find that he didn't really mind too much about having been eliminated – he'd just had the greatest time with his mates and nothing could have spoiled that.

As it was almost lunchtime, they decided to look for somewhere to eat. Satras had filled up even more since that morning and Julius was taken aback by all the different nationalities of the people around him. He found that comforting and was sure that Marcus Tijara would have loved to have seen his dream of a united Earth come true.

They were about to step onto one of the bridges when Faith suddenly stopped: 'Look guys, it's Pit-Stop Pete! I'm gonna go thank him for the skirt.'

They were quite happy to join him and take a closer look at this famous character of Zed. However, as they drew nearer, they realised that Pete was locked in deep conversation with two other men, and he seemed quite upset. They stopped a little distance away, waiting for him to finish. Julius caught a glimpse of a black wisp rising from Pete's head. He shook his head slightly and the wisp disappeared – he didn't need his powers to see that Pete was having an argument. One of the men, who was wearing a red cap down to his brow, stood in front of Pete with a calm, almost mocking expression on his face. Julius felt that something was not quite right about him.

'He feels ... different,' he thought, although how so, he couldn't say.

Eventually the men left and Pete remained there, shaking his head. Faith advanced slowly towards the old man and the group followed him.

'Excuse me, sir,' said Faith timidly.

The full head of candid, white hair turned suddenly around. As soon as he saw the skirt his face lit up.

'Mr Shanigan,' he said in his pleasant drawl. 'How good t' see ya out an' about.'

'I don't know how to thank you for me gift,' said Faith blushing, 'but it means the world to me.'

Pete's smile widened.

'Then I'm even gladder I made it, son. Nothing can come between us an' our dreams. You remember that.'

'He sure will,' said Morgana, moving forward. 'He just won his first race in the Palace!'

'Is that right? Wanna be a pilot?'

'Morgana is the pilot really. I want to build Zed's spaceships,' answered Faith, with more confidence in his voice.

'I'm sure you will. But be prepared, in this here line o' work ya'll have to swallow a lotta dirt, kid.'

'You mean like the two guys that you were talking to?' asked Julius earnestly.

Morgana nudged him in the ribs and he realised that he had been too forward.

'I'm sorry, I didn't mean to …'

'It's all right, son,' cut in Pete kindly. 'My dockin' base is always full an' very busy. The last thing I need's a ship parked there for no reason, takin' up precious space, unloadin' stock that's not even for me. But that's how the Curia wants it, an' there ain't nothin' I can do about it. That's what I mean by dirt. Well, don't you go worryin' about it, now. You enjoy your new gadget, Mr Shanigan, an' I'm sure I'll see ya soon for a little work experience, right?'

Faith nodded enthusiastically and shook his hand with evident admiration. Pete waved to them all and hobbled off into the crowd. Julius followed him with his eyes. Pete had tried to dismiss the incident, but the black wisp had reappeared above his head.

THE HOLOPAL

The opening of the game season had sent Julius and his classmates into a frenzy as they looked to spend as much time as possible in the Hologram Palace. Students were allowed in Satras every day, although they had a curfew of eight pm from Sunday to Thursday and nine pm on Fridays and Saturdays. The Skirts – they had unanimously decided to keep the name that had brought them such good luck in their first game – had managed to squeeze in several sessions after classes, as training for the weekend. At Julius's suggestion, they had agreed to concentrate on racing games for that year and to play only against each other during their weekly training. The extra practice had paid off, as over the following weekends their stats had improved greatly among the 1 Mizki players. To Faith's immense pleasure, Billy Somers's name was nowhere to be seen in the charts.

The Skirts's quick rise to fame had even been noticed by Professor Clavel, who had made several positive remarks during their pilot training lessons. One such afternoon, Julius and his classmates were logging off from their computer terminals, concluding a hard day of work on basic engine maintenance theory.

'Your attention, Mizki,' said Clavel to the class. 'How many of you have used the race simulation games?'

A forest of arms quickly shot up. Julius looked around and noticed that only four girls and Barth, Faith's roommate, had not put their hands up.

'As a *suggestion*,' continued Clavel, 'I would recommend that everyone get at least a few games under their belts before the end of term. Our first flight sim-lesson in school won't be until February and a little experience will be greatly advantageous.' With that he looked directly at Julius and his team mates. 'I have noticed that some among you have taken a particular liking to racing games. Isn't that right, Miss Ruthier?'

'Yes sir!' answered Morgana, evidently delighted at the direct acknowledgement from a teacher.

'I am very pleased,' answered Clavel. 'Incidentally, how did you come up with your team name?'

Morgana blushed and looked over at Faith.

'It was a good, good friend of ours who suggested it, sir. We didn't want to disappoint him,' answered Faith, with one of his trademark grins.

Clavel nodded and dismissed the class, ignoring the fact that both Julius and Skye could barely contain their laughter.

Unfortunately, as they went deeper into November, Julius noticed a sudden increase in the level of homework they were receiving from their teachers. The game practices had to be cut to twice a week, since most evenings they were either mapping the Milky Way in the library or practising their draws until they had finally run out of cactus plants.

The Martial Arts lessons had become more and more exhausting. Professor Chan had set a fixed routine schedule for the students until the end of term. On Tuesday afternoons, they would run countless laps around the dojo, lift weights and do umpteen push-ups and pull-ups until their arms and legs gave in. On Wednesdays, Chan made them practice Mindkatas for the entire three hours. Following a brief warm up, Julius would face a holographic target and practice his katas against it until the target was eliminated and immediately replaced by a new one. He had to channel his powers through his legs and arms, in sets of one hundred per limb. Then, he would restart the cycle all over again. One time he was so exhausted after training that he fell asleep in the changing room shower, and it was only because Skye had found him twenty minutes later that his skin hadn't completely prunified. After that, the Skirts decided unanimously to cancel game practice on Tuesdays and Wednesdays.

'Heck,' said Skye that afternoon, as they lay sprawled out under the oak tree in the garden, 'I can't even lift my pen to write in my diary, never mind convincing my legs to carry me as far as Satras.'

'I hear you,' added Faith. 'Julius, you might have fallen asleep in the shower today, but last night I fell asleep in me skirt, standing like a horse. Unfortunately Barth decided to wake me up, but given his still appalling knowledge of the room control panel, instead of switching the light on he got the bed out of the wall, which rammed into me waist and sent me wheeling against the wall!'

'Oh boy,' said Morgana, with a snort, 'did you hurt yourself?'

'Nah, but Barth was mortified. He couldn't stop apologising. He's a bit of a menace that one. I don't know if I would trust him with a shopping trolley, never mind a space ship.'

'Maybe you could invite him to practise with us sometime,' said Julius.

'Yeah, maybe – when I'm feeling suicidal!'

One Monday morning, after a breakfast of honey-poached figs and spicy potato cakes, Julius made his way to the White Arts sector. Since the beginning of term, he had arrived later and later in the mess hall and often the others would already have left by the time he had finished his breakfast. He really couldn't get himself out of bed early, but since he had never been late for class, no one had ever complained. Monday mornings had also become the worst days for Julius. Although he liked Professor Lao-tzu very much, Meditation was his least favourite subject. He felt that achieving a perfect meditative state in less than a minute was way beyond his abilities. He had tried to change the landscape to see if it would help, but in the end the stone tower on top of the hill had proven to be the only place where he really felt comfortable. Neither Faith nor Skye had managed to go below the time limit, but they had achieved a brief meditative state nonetheless. He didn't even want to consider Morgana, who could get into a trance in 57 seconds, setting the record for the whole class.

As he descended to the classroom that morning, he found his classmates already kneeling on the floor in a circle waiting for Lao-tzu. He squeezed between Morgana and Skye and prepared himself for another dreadful performance. A few minutes later the professor entered the room, kneeled and bowed to the students. He was carrying a small leather box, which he placed on the floor in front of him.

'Good morning to you all,' he said in his usual tranquil voice. 'Before we begin our practice, I would like to introduce you to a very interesting device.' As he said that, he opened the box and lifted out an object similar to a hair band, but made entirely of glass. At its extremities were two pea sized spheres.

'This is a Scrambler, a device built by Clodagh Arnesh herself when she was still a teacher in Tijara.'

The class fell silent and Julius found himself leaning in slightly towards Lao-tzu.

'As you know, Clodagh Arnesh did not possess a single White Art skill. However, she was a genius when it came to technology. It was she who created the Grey Arts. Her friend Marcus Tijara had it all: he was a natural talent with all the White Arts and a very apt pupil when it came to learning the Grey ones. Arnesh felt incomplete compared to him. So she decided that, if she could not master both Arts, she would be the only one who could access the full potential of the Grey Arts. She became paranoid that Marcus, or anyone else with similar abilities, would read her mind and steal her technological secrets. It was at that time that she invented the Scrambler, a machine that creates a field of high frequency interference within the mind of the wearer, making telesthesia practically impossible.'

'Sir,' said Lopaka Liway, 'what is telesthesia?'

'It is a rare White Art ability that lets you perceive the thoughts of people around you, among other things, without the use of your normal sensory system. As well as blocking an outsider from reading your thoughts, the Scrambler was also devised to confuse the minds of those who came near it, which brings us back to meditation. As you work towards your goal of achieving relaxation, trance and balance, you effectively minimise the risks of being affected by one of these gadgets. You will have a chance to practice with Scramblers, once you have achieved your time limit goal.' Lao-tzu then stood and invited the students to choose their landscape for the day.

Julius walked automatically towards the top right corner of the room, sat down on his screen and closed his eyes. His mind was fully distracted by the Scramblers and by what Lao-tzu had said about telesthesia. It was a rare skill, but had he not experienced it many times before? It had always happened unintentionally and for brief spells, but he had been able to do it. He also knew that, when he did perceive other people's thoughts, he always felt very relaxed.

'If only I could figure out how to recreate that relaxation,' he thought.

However, the more he tried the tenser he became, and by the end of the lesson he was utterly depressed. Unfortunately, a new set of worries was about to settle on the class. Before leaving, Professor Lao-tzu asked them to stay behind a few more minutes. Tony Tower entered the room, bowed to the students and kneeled before them.

'Mizki, I have been sent to inform you that you are all up for review this week.'

The entire class let out a collective gasp at those words.

'Every November and June,' continued Tower, 'all Tijaran students meet with the heads of their year. They will discuss your progress with you and the subjects that you need to improve on. Where necessary, extra work will be assigned. As you know, there are no exams at the end of each year, but you are still required to demonstrate your proficiency in all first and second year courses if you want to continue your life on Zed. After today's lessons, there will be a schedule for the meetings in the school lounge at level -3. Find your name and the date of your appointment. Whatever you do, don't be late. Class dismissed.'

Julius felt a cold shiver run down his spine. For all the progress he had made since August, Meditation was still his Achilles' heel and he knew that his review would suffer for it. As the afternoon crawled on, that sense of chill had not left him and, when the last class ended, he rushed to the lounge unable to contain himself any longer. As he entered, Julius realised that he had rarely been in that area since arriving on Tijara. It was softly lit, filled with comfortable sofas and armchairs. A fireplace occupied the far wall – it was large enough that it could easily have fitted five students standing abreast. The large windows around the room were in fact scenery screens and, as Julius looked at them, he noticed that it had begun to snow. On the right hand side of the entrance, a set of stairs led to the underground levels. As he made his way down, a buzz of students' voices rose up to meet him. He realised that the students were all Mizki Seniors, judging by their height, and that Tony Tower and Bernard Docherty were among them. He kept going, throwing just a glance at the people gathered on level -2.

'Those must be the 3 and 4 Mizki Apprentices,' thought Julius, without stopping. Finally he arrived at the Juniors' level. A large group of 2MJ were already huddled against the wall, looking for their names on the list. He tried to peek over their shoulders, but he was still too far away to read anything.

'There you are Julius,' said Faith, appearing suddenly behind him. 'You must have been very keen to get down here.'

'Faith,' said Julius, pulling him closer, 'can you lift us above them?'

'Sure. Hop on.'

Julius climbed the rim of the Skirt and held on to Faith as they hovered slowly upwards. The other students were pushing and pulling below them, hitting the Skirt as they tried to protect their heads from Faith's feet.

'I found the first year's schedule,' said Julius stretching his neck towards the list.

'Good, so you can read mine too. I'm kinda struggling to keep us still, here.'

'Smock … Slovich … Shanigan! Your appointment is tomorrow at noon in the office, level -1 with Mrs Cruci. Same for me, except I'll see her at 12:30. OK, get us down Faith.'

Faith landed them in the centre of the lounge and they made their way to the mess hall. When Morgana and Skye joined them for tea, Julius was almost relieved to discover that they too were feeling as tense as he was. No one felt like going to Satras – instead they spent their evening in the garden, looking through their school diaries and discussing their individual performances in the various subjects. By the time he went to bed that night, Julius was a little more relaxed, comforted by the fact that at least he wasn't alone in his worries.

The following morning, Julius's class was unusually quiet. All the students were feeling very nervous as their individual meetings approached. A little before midday, Faith left the Draw class to attend his appointment. Morgana's review had been earlier that morning, but Julius had not been able to discuss it with her since Professor Turner had kept them busy drawing from saplings.

Julius didn't feel like eating before his meeting with Mrs Cruci so, when the lesson ended, he walked over to the office and sat on the long circular bench that surrounded the fountain around the assembly hall. Morgana joined him shortly afterwards.

'I thought you might be here,' she said, sitting down next to him. 'How did your meeting go?'

'It was fine, I guess. Mrs Cruci is a really nice woman and made me feel completely at ease. In general I'm doing all right. I have to improve in Draw and make more effort in Martial Arts, but I'm top of the class in Meditation.'

'No surprise there. You always had a knack for it,' said Julius, looking down at his feet.

'Is Meditation what's troubling you?'

'Yeah … and I don't know how to make it better. Morgana, how do you slip into a trance so quickly?'

'Practice, I guess.'

'Yes, but what *exactly* do you do?'

'Well, you concentrate on something so completely that you stop being aware of anything else, even yourself,' she answered evenly.

'But if you're not aware of yourself, how do you know? I mean, once you realise you're in a trance then surely you are also aware of yourself?'

'For one, I don't ask myself if I'm in a trance or not. I just *feel* it and I stay there, until I'm calm and relaxed.'

Julius nodded, but he was still worried.

'Mrs Cruci will help you, I'm sure. Besides, Julius, you're one of the best in every other subject. It's unlikely they'll kick you out of Zed. Listen,' she said, standing up, 'I'm going to have some food now. Before you enter, take a deep breath and calm down. You'll be fine.'

Julius watched her leave, then stood up and approached the office area. Quietly, he opened the main door and entered. Inside was a corridor that ended in a window overlooking Tijara's main entrance. The waterfall outside fashioned a curtain of rain against the glass, creating wavy reflections on the marble floor. To the left of the window, a set of stairs led downwards, presumably to the lower levels. There were two doors to either side of the corridor, and Julius gasped when he saw the name plaque on the right hand door – behind that, the Grand Master Tijara was sitting at his desk.

Julius had just begun to wonder if Freja knew about his dreadful performance in Meditation, when the other door opened. He turned on his heels in a flash and found himself staring at Master Cress.

'Good afternoon, Mr McCoy. Step inside my office please.'

Julius was so taken aback by the sudden appearance of Cress that he didn't know what to do.

'Sir, I have a meeting with Mrs Cruci in a short while.'

'I know. However, Mrs Cruci must attend to other business as soon as she is finished with Mr Shanigan; therefore I shall do your review in her place.'

Julius's heartbeat instantly went from a canter to a gallop at that news. There was nothing he could do, though, but follow Cress into his office. As he sat, he noticed several framed pictures on the wall, each containing younger versions of Cress as he made his career in Zed. He smiled at one of the pictures because, if he wasn't mistaken, there was a Mizki Junior Cress standing in the centre of it, flanked by two others boys. Julius followed the sequence on the wall: Cress holding a trophy outside the Hologram Palace; graduating from Tijara; shaking hands with Freja; being made Master; sitting inside a jet plane, a huge smile on his face.

'I feel as if those pictures were taken only yesterday,' said Cress quietly.

Julius was almost positive that Cress wasn't particularly old, so seeing all that he had accomplished in such a short period of time, left him slightly in awe of the Master.

'You must have been very determined, sir,' said Julius before he'd even had time to consider whether or not it was appropriate to make such a remark.

'And you are not, Mr McCoy?' replied Cress, staring intently at him. 'I heard from your teachers that you are, and that is always a good start, especially when certain problems need to be addressed.'

Julius didn't know what to say, so he simply nodded, hoping that Cress would put him out of his misery as soon as possible. The Master activated his desk. Its flat, glass face was soon filled with information, menus and buttons, all moving slowly across its surface. Cress pressed one of the menus and instantly Julius's file opened. He read the report quietly for a few minutes, before looking up at Julius.

'I see you have taken quite a fancy to racing games, Mr McCoy. You and your team have made impressive progress in the game world. All that after-school training has definitely paid off.'

'Thank you, sir,' said Julius, pleasantly surprised. He had not expected Cress to take any interest in the students' out of school activities.

'Game achievements are monitored by teachers,' said Cress, as if he had read Julius's mind. 'We can tell a lot about our students by the way they behave during them – combat and flight skills, leadership, they all count towards forming a complete individual. Moreover, the fact that you have enough Fyvers to play and practise means that your performance in class must also be good. You eat healthily and regularly enough and your body is in good shape, according to Professor Chan. This is also important. *Mens sana in corpore sano*. It's Latin, and it means "a healthy mind in a healthy body". Never forget that. You have a regular sleep pattern, normal for a developing boy such as yourself. That said, I can see that you do rather like to wake up at the last possible minute.'

Julius shifted uncomfortably in his chair. He'd thought that Cress would only be discussing his subjects with him but instead he felt completely exposed, as if there was nothing he could do without the whole of Tijara knowing about it.

'All of your teachers have been satisfied with your performance so far, all except one. Do you know who might that be?'

'Professor Lao-tzu, sir?' answered Julius sheepishly.

'Correct. Your teacher has told me that you have not been able to achieve any sort of meditative state as yet. You seem restless and out of focus when you enter his class. Does this reflect your feelings for Professor Lao-tzu, Mr McCoy?'

'Not at all, sir. I like him very much. I just …' Julius tried to express how he felt, but no words came to his mouth.

Cress looked at him for a moment, then spoke into his headset: 'Mr List, this is Master Cress. Please ready a holopal for Mr McCoy, 1MJ, by the end of today. I shall send you the configuration within the hour.'

Julius looked at Cress with a puzzled expression.

'You must defeat this obstacle, Mr McCoy. The holopal is a program designed specifically for helping students overcome any subject related difficulties. You shall have morning meetings with your holopal, Monday to Friday, starting from tomorrow. You will meet in one of the hologram rooms between 05:00 and 07:00. If you are ever late, you will be given detention. On Monday mornings, you will study Meditation with your classmates, as usual. I am giving you until the end of February. If there are still no improvements, we will perhaps have to reconsider your training on Zed. Am I clear, Mr McCoy?'

'Sir, yes, sir,' said Julius, devastated. He couldn't believe his ears. For a start, he really wasn't a morning person. Plus, Morgana had just told him that no one could kick him out of Tijara for having trouble in one subject, yet here he was, having just been given an ultimatum by Master Cress himself.

'The holopal can be configured to look like anyone you wish,' continued Cress seriously. 'Normally a shape that is conducive to your aim, in this case, achieving relaxation and a meditative state. Now, Mr McCoy, I read in your file that you are quite passionate about Earth history and have a keen interest in Japanese culture, am I right?'

'Yes sir,' answered Julius promptly.

'In that case, I suggest a Zen master to be your holopal. As a matter of fact, we have already used this specific shape in the past, with successful results. Will you give it a try?'

Julius nodded.

'Very well, Mr McCoy. Report to Mr List tonight at 20:00 hours. You are free to go now.'

'Thank you, sir,' said Julius, standing up. He bowed to Cress and left his office.

'I still can't believe you had your review with Cress.' said Skye, clearly dumbstruck.

Julius had met up with the others in the garden, after their Martial Arts lesson. He had told them all about his meeting and the holopal.

'Were any of you given remedial classes?' asked Julius rather miserably.

Morgana looked at Faith and Skye, and by their looks Julius knew that the answer was no.

'Great. I bet I'm the only one in our year that was.'

'So what?' said Morgana. 'It's only until February anyway. By then, I'm sure you'll be fine. Besides it shows that they care about us. It's their job to make us the best that we can be.'

'I think Morgana is right,' said Faith. 'I mean about the caring stuff. I might not have remedial classes, but … they put me on a diet … from chocolate …'

'What?' said Skye. 'But you're skinny, man!'

'Well, it's for the Skirt. I need to check me weight, so that I can still fit in this thing. Also, pilots' chairs are not that big and, with all the different pressures and null gravity and the like, being fit is kinda compulsory.'

The image of a fat blob walking around in the Skirt made Julius smile. 'I guess you're right and, anyway, there's nothing I can do about it.'

They spent the rest of the afternoon lazing around on the grass, filling in their diaries and discussing new racing strategies. As the sun set, they went inside for their meal, after which Julius took his leave.

'You gotta tell me everything about the holopal when you get back,' said Faith excitedly.

'For sure, I'll catch you guys later.'

Julius left the mess hall and made his way to the holographic sector. When he got there, Gabriel List was sitting at the front desk.

'Mr McCoy,' he said in an official tone of voice, 'follow me please.'

They went down to level -1, where List stopped outside a door marked "Technician's Den". He looked at the retinal scanner and the door opened. The "den" was effectively a staff room for List and his colleagues, and was by far the most chaotic room Julius had seen anywhere inside the school. Tiny little robots whisked around the floor, picking up pieces of paper, gum wrappers and fluffs of dust. The many shelves surrounding the room were crammed with beeping silver gadgets, whose function totally escaped Julius. He noticed that the walls were actually writing screens, filled with mathematical equations and scarily long formulae.

'Don't mind the mess,' said List, kicking one of the robots out of his way. 'We seem to concentrate better in this environment.'

Julius smiled as he watched a robot the size of his foot attempting to pick up a peanut butter sandwich that was practically glued to the floor.

'My friend Faith would love this room.'

'Is he the guy with Pete's Skirt?' asked List, ushering Julius into a smaller, empty room.

'Yes. He's very good with gadgets and the like.'

'Maybe I should invite him over sometime.'

'He'd like that, sir.'

'In here you can call me Gabriel. Zed is far too formal for my taste.' He gave Julius a big smile and guided him into one of the classrooms.

'I've received Cress's configuration for a Zen master and I took the liberty of doing a little research on the topic in order to find you a suitable one. I want you to try it out. Remember, the holopal is state of the art VI – virtual intelligence – it thinks, it has a nanosecond reaction time to process info, it makes decisions and can physically interact with its surroundings.' List pulled a watch out of his pocket and gave it to Julius. 'Put it on, and when you are ready I want you to place your finger on the centre of the screen.'

Julius followed the instructions and an old Japanese man appeared, kneeling opposite him.

'Let me introduce you to Master Isshin,' said List, retreating quietly out of the room.

Julius stared at the man, unable to say a word. He couldn't read the expression on his face. Isshin seemed to possess both the tranquillity of Lao-tzu and the sharpness of Chan. His eyes were small and dark, but penetrating. He wore a blue kimono over his bent, aged body. Julius shifted uncomfortably, wondering if he was supposed to say or do something. Suddenly the man lifted a hand and waved it in the air between them. The familiar sensation of displacement that Julius felt whenever he sat atop his tower in Lao-tzu's class swept over him, as he found himself in a forest in the early evening dusk. Isshin stood effortlessly and gestured for Julius to follow him. As he walked behind the master, Julius breathed in, enjoying the smell of the evening around him and the moss of the trees. A small wooden temple appeared just ahead of them, with four pillars holding up a pagoda-style roof. Isshin led him towards it. Julius removed his boots outside the entrance, as the master removed his shoes. A white tatami covered the floor, with two rows of cushions on it. Sticks of sandalwood incense were burning swiftly, permeating the air around them.

'Please sit in the lotus position, Mr McCoy.'

Isshin's voice was friendly and surprisingly young, thought Julius. He followed the instruction as best as he could, but lost his balance trying to cross his legs in the appropriate fashion.

'Perhaps the half lotus will do for now,' said Isshin, easing into that position himself. 'I want you to keep your spine relaxed but straight, and your head level. Your eyes must remain half closed, to avoid falling asleep.'

Julius thought that between the warm, lulling air, the sweet incense and that afternoon's Martial Arts lesson, there was no way he would stay awake, so he was more than happy when Master Isshin continued to talk.

'What do you know about Zen, Mr McCoy?'

'It's a Japanese form of Buddhism, where meditation is very important.'

'You are quite correct. Professor Lao-tzu's methods are successful with most students. However, for some the practice of more ancient methods is best, which is why you are here. Using meditation, Zen Buddhists would try to achieve enlightenment, a flash of insight, an awakening of the mind beyond logical comprehension. Interestingly, these *satori*, these flashes, seem to come during everyday activities, when the mind is relaxed, rather than when one is trying too hard to concentrate.'

Julius's eyes widened imperceptibly, but still enough for Master Isshin to notice.

'I believe, Mr McCoy, that you have experienced telesthesia before, am I right?'

'Yes sir. I have never done it on purpose though. It just happens.'

'That is a strength,' said Isshin, 'and we are going to use it to our advantage. Tell me, what happens within you as you sit on top of the tower?'

'I breathe deeply, close my eyes and try to clear away all thoughts,' answered Julius. 'It doesn't work though. Either my thoughts get more chaotic or I fall asleep.'

Master Isshin nodded. 'If you are looking at a pool of clear water and someone throws a handful of dirt in it, what would be the quickest way to restore its clearness?'

'Not to touch it?' said Julius tentatively.

'Correct. You let it settle by itself. If you stir it, or try to move it away, it may never do that. During our sessions, I want you to do just that. Don't fight away your thoughts, but follow them, observe them, relax with them. They are part of you.'

Julius nodded.

'Very well, Mr McCoy. I shall meet you here tomorrow morning at 05:00. You can deactivate me by touching your watch whenever you are ready to leave.'

Julius felt quite awkward. He knew that Isshin wasn't real and he could just switch him off at will, but somehow that just didn't feel right. In the end he stood and bowed respectfully to the master, before touching his watch. Walking out of the hologram sector, he felt a little confidence returning, as this new method seemed to be more fitting for him. Frankly, given the choice between waking at the crack of dawn and being thrown of out of Zed, he knew which one to choose, even if it meant sleeping in the Technician's Den.

GOING SOLO

As Julius entered the last week of November, he had never felt more tired in his whole life. The homework had doubled in all subjects and Professor Chan continued to train them as hard as if they were an Olympic team. He had to abandon his cosy bed at an outrageous hour, while Skye would be snoring peacefully from under his blanket. The thought that he could only have breakfast after two hours of staring at trees and bees during meditation made his stomach rumble and his temper rise. On top of all this, Professor Turner started to observe Julius's draws a little too closely for his liking. She would try to be casual about it – tiptoeing around behind his back, looking over his shoulder – but Julius wasn't fooled. He knew that, ever since his first draw attempt, her interest in his ability had increased significantly, even though he wasn't quite sure why.

At last, after an excruciating session of Martial Arts, he approached his mates in the mess hall and made a painful announcement: 'I'm sorry, guys. I'll have to give up the weekly training for a little while.'

'Frankly I'm surprised you've lasted so long, man,' said Faith over his carrot salad.

Julius dropped down onto a chair with his head in his hands.

'… nasty alarm is killing me …'

'Don't worry about it,' said Skye. 'We all have tonnes of homework anyway.'

'Besides, I'm sure you'll master meditation long before the winter break,' added Morgana, trying to sound cheerful.

'Will I? Really?' asked Julius, frustrated. 'The way I see it, that holopal of mine is not really doing what it's supposed to. I think it's so bored by the whole thing that it's started to flicker on me on purpose – which is very upsetting by the way. This morning it disappeared after dragging me to the top of Mount Fuji. I had to wait an hour before Gabriel List realised something was wrong and rescued me. Perched on that peak like a bird and all I could think of was blinking bacon and eggs!'

They stared at him for a moment before bursting into laughter. Julius couldn't help but join in. They spent the rest of the evening in the Juniors' lounge helping each other with an essay on the Galilean Moons, trying to figure out which one was which.

'I'm telling you,' said Faith waving his pencil at Skye, 'the big one is Callisto!'

'But Callisto is all dark and this is kinda lightish,' answered Skye, shoving a picture under Faith's nose.

'Then it must be Europa.'

'Can't be,' added Julius. 'It's far too big.'

They all looked at Morgana, as if waiting for the right answer.

'What?' she said, peering over her book. 'What are you looking at me for?'

'Well, you're the pilot,' said Skye. 'You're supposed to know.'

Morgana shook her head and grabbed the picture from Skye's hand.

'It's Ganymede. It's got dark patches and lighter grooves and it's the largest moon in the Solar System.'

'That settles it,' said Faith matter of factly. 'That leaves Io, the yellow one.'

'That's sulphur,' added Morgana vaguely.

'It could be me grandmother's custard for all I care. I'm too tired, guys. I'm gonna call it a night.'

'Hear, hear!' said Skye, packing up.

Julius agreed wholeheartedly and followed them back to the dormitories. Unfortunately, he was so looking forward to his bed that he forgot to set the alarm. At 05:00 hours, the lights in the room came on. Julius sprung up from the bed, blurry eyed. Skye was fast asleep and, in the corridor, all was silent. Suddenly his eyes widened in a mixture of surprise and fear.

'Oh no, I'm dead!' he kept repeating aloud as he jumped out of bed and scooped his clothes from the floor. He flew out of the room and up the stairs, trying to shove his head through one of the sleeves of his jumper as he went. The main corridor was empty and he ran as fast as he could, doing his best to ignore the smell of breakfast coming from the mess hall. When he finally arrived at the hologram sector, the door was closed. He only just managed to slow down before he could crash into the wall. It was then that he saw the note on the door:

"Mr McCoy,

Arriving late for the morning sessions was NOT in the agreement. You shall spend your afternoon in the detention room in the library.

Master Cress."

'I was only a few minutes late!' shouted Julius at the door. 'It's not fair!'

Nobody answered him, however. The only noise in the corridor was that of the waterfall trickling over the black marble wall of the assembly room. Dejectedly, he headed over to the mess hall.

'At least I'm getting an early breakfast this morning,' he thought, trying unconvincingly to cheer himself up.

A couple of hours later, Julius was awoken by Morgana and realised that he had fallen asleep on one of the benches in the canteen.

She sat down next to him and shook him gently by the shoulder. 'You don't look too happy. What's up?'

Julius rubbed his eyes and told her what had happened.

'How can he do this? I've never been late before!'

'Come on Julius, don't be mad. There's no point really. Look what I brought you,' she said, rummaging in her bag and handing him a chip. 'It's my relaxing music collection. I thought it might help you get into the right frame of mind.'

'Thanks Morgana,' he said, feeling slightly less grumpy.

'I made a copy, so you can keep that one.'

'I might use it for my afternoon detention. You never know.'

'Let's get some breakfast now. I'm starving,' she said, dragging him by the arm.

As with every Thursday, his only class was three hours of Telekinesis in the morning. Julius thoroughly enjoyed these lessons with Professor King, seeing as he was quite good at this subject. That, however, meant that time passed even quicker and before he knew it he found himself outside the library for his detention.

Miss Evelyne Dubois was the young librarian who welcomed Julius at the door. Students were allowed in this particular section of the microchip library only with special permission or, as in this case, for detention. The room was cosy and welcoming, simply furnished, with slick black terminals attached to ten separate mahogany desks. There were four other senior students in the room with him and they all looked up briefly as he entered the room and walked over to one of the empty desks. With a big sigh, he pulled out his diary, deciding that he would use the time to update his daily progress. He also took out Morgana's music chip to listen to.

After two hours of solid work, Julius put his pen down and looked up towards Miss Dubois. He wasn't sure how long his detention was supposed to last for and, as he was about to go and ask, his eyes fell on a stack of chips at the bottom of a shelf. The label above them simply read "Draw". Julius suddenly remembered the conversation he had with Skye about Tijara's notes on the subject. He had never gotten around to checking them out as he had been meaning to do. He scanned the chips quickly until he came across one labelled "Marcus Tijara and the White Art of Drawing". He saw that Miss Dubois was busy talking with a student and was facing the door. Carefully, Julius picked up the chip and inserted it into a slot in the side of the monitor.

Julius scanned through the various chapters. He knew most of the information from his lessons, but kept reading. Eventually he found a short chapter called "Drawing from inorganic matter". In it, Marcus Tijara explained how it was still a largely unexplored field with only a handful of recorded case studies. Despite the lack of documented evidence, however, it was indeed possible. Only once had Tijara come across a subject who had been able to perform a draw from a microwave oven. The subject had later discharged a small electric shock upon touching a metal object. Julius's eyes widened at that. Suddenly the memory of his first draw flooded back to him and, with it, the image of Professor Turner's digital watch, stopped, on her wrist. What if he had actually caused the watch to stop? Had he really drawn from it? The energy receiver had been charged to the full, but his cactus had not withered. Where had that energy come from? Julius looked back at the screen. Tijara said that the subject had released an electric shock onto a metal object. He remembered clearly how he had touched the door handle of Miss Turner's classroom and how it had flown out of his hand, slamming against the wall as if pushed by an unseen force. His heartbeat quickened and he continued reading:

"Shortly after this episode, the subject's health deteriorated at a dramatic rate. His body went into shock and eventually shut down completely before we could intervene. We could only watch as his skin started to burn from the inside. It was as if a bolt of lightning had entered his body and stayed there. He died almost immediately. Although an isolated event, this dreadful experience has at least confirmed that inorganic drawing is possible. If another human should be able to recreate this act, he or she would be strongly advised to discharge the energy as soon as possible, in order to avoid a similar fate to that of our test subject. We are in no position to know if, in case of survival, the subject would have suffered or developed side-effects. What we do know is that, like the other subjects capable of inorganic drawing, all his White skills were incredibly powerful. Finally, as a word of caution, if another individual with this power is discovered, they should be brought to the attention of the Grand Masters as a security measure."

Julius slumped back in his chair. It was all so difficult to believe, but deep down he had no doubts. He was now certain that he had drawn from a lifeless object.

'Mr McCoy,' called Miss Dubois from her desk.

Julius almost jumped out of his chair at that, engrossed as he was in his thoughts.

'Your detention is over. You can leave now.'

Julius switched off the monitor and placed the chip back on the shelf. He left the library without looking up, not knowing where to go. He felt strangely alone, as if the discovery of his ability had placed him in an empty slot, isolating him somehow from his friends. Yet he felt that he needed them now more than ever. He wasn't sure if he would tell them about Tijara's chip, but he did know he needed their company right then. He searched the dorms, the lounge and the garden, but couldn't find any of them. Frustrated, he walked towards the exit, thinking that they might have gone to Satras. He boarded the Intra-Rail System, oblivious of the students laughing around him. All he could think of were the last words written by Tijara, about how anyone like him should be reported for security. What was he to do? Tell Cress? What if they asked him to leave Zed? He couldn't bear that. As he stepped off the main lift inside Satras, and started to walk beside the lake, a thought came to him which made him feel a little more hopeful. The day he had drawn from Professor Turner's watch, she had been standing over him. She knew exactly what Julius had done and, no doubt, had reported her findings. Yet, no one had ever talked to him about it, as if it wasn't important at all.

'Well,' Julius said to himself, 'if they aren't bothered, then neither am I.'

Dismissing his fears, Julius stopped and looked around, but

there was still no trace of Morgana or the others. He realised that he was standing outside the Hologram Palace and decided to check inside before going back to Tijara. In the arena, there were only a few students sitting on the large steps and most of the game screens were inactive. He checked the boards but the Skirts's names weren't on any of them either. As he was walking past the booking kiosk, a wrinkled old hand shot out and grabbed him by the arm. Julius almost let out a scream and staggered backwards.

'Heeee! Sorry lad. Didn't mean to scare you.'

Julius looked up at old Mrs Mayflower, startled. He had seen her quite regularly since he had started playing and couldn't believe that someone with so many wrinkles could actually have enough energy for such a fast movement.

'It's all right. I was distracted. I ... can I help you?'

'I thought you just needed a little encouragement,' she said with a smile.

'For what?'

'But for playing Solo of course, my dear. Why else would you be walking this empty courtyard without your team?'

'Actually, I wasn't really ...'

'Come, come lad. I have been running this kiosk for 60 years. I have seen plenty of young hopeful students coming this way, in the middle of the week, alone, looking for a shot at glory,' she said with a knowing wink. 'Take young Mr Docherty for instance – he came here when he was a 3 Mizki Apprentice. A scrawny little thing he was, a little taller than you perhaps. He arrived alone, on a midweek evening, just like you. And from that moment, his life changed. He made it into the top ten Solo records, at number one. The first new blood in fifty years!' she clapped her old hands together delightedly, as if speaking of the past made her feel young again. 'So, Julius lad, what will you do?'

'About what?'

'Eeeeh! I thought you were smart. Taking a shot at Solo. What else?'

'No, really. I ... I don't think it's a good idea at all.'

'Come on. No one will know. If you don't make it into the top ten, your name won't even appear on the board. You have nothing to lose.'

Julius thought about it for a moment. To tell the truth, he was really curious about Solo. He had wanted to try it ever since his arrival on Zed and, given that he was on his own, and still trying to digest what he had learned in the library, perhaps it wasn't a bad idea after all.

'All right, sign me in.'

'One Solo ticket coming up! Go through the right door and good luck.'

Julius thanked her and made his way to the entrance, throwing one last glance over his shoulder to check that nobody had seen him. He followed the stairs down to a small room, where a man was sitting behind a desk reading a comic book. He looked up as Julius entered.

'Hey, the first customer of the day. Come in!'

Julius walked forward, trying not to look too scared.

'Hi, I'm Mr Preston. First time, huh?'

'Is it that obvious?'

'Don't worry, I've seen worse.'

'So, what do I do?'

'Well, you get your holosuit in the changing room and then

wait to be called, like in the group games. I'll set you up. The main difference in Solo is that you don't get to choose your challenge against the simulator. You could be racing, or you could be fighting, or both, and you *will* be using your actual mind-skills. The difficulty level has been the same since Marcus Tijara's time. Just so you know, it was him and that traitor Arnesh, may she rot in space, who built this Palace.'

'How difficult is it?'

'Pretty nasty, but don't worry – you can't actually die. There's a safety protocol written into the program. Right this way then,' he said, ushering Julius into the dressing room.

Julius was given a holosuit, exactly like the one he used for the group games, and an object that looked like a glass mask, with a thick rubber rim around its edge.

'This is a face shield,' said Preston. 'Put it on when I tell you to. It will allow you to breathe. Good luck.'

Julius nodded and started to undress. He looked apprehensively at the face shield and wondered why he would need any kind of breathing device at all. A few minutes later he was called to make his way through the green door.

The Solo area itself seemed really small compared to the group game floor, and very different. There were no holospheres to begin with, but instead Julius counted twenty cubic tanks, which looked much like aquariums, each one as big as his bedroom. Preston motioned him towards the first of the containers where they stepped onto a platform which raised them both to the top of the tank. Julius peered into it and saw that it was filled with a transparent jelly-like substance.

'Put your shield on now,' said Preston.

Julius felt a slight suction as its rim closed around his face. He tried to breathe but it was oddly difficult and was just about to take off the mask when Preston pushed him unceremoniously into the tank. He slid into the clear jelly, feeling very much like a tadpole slinking its way through mud.

'Can you hear me?' said Preston, his voice now slightly muffled.

Julius looked up and nodded.

'Great. Take a deep breath.'

Julius did and the oxygen entered his lungs immediately, slowing his heartbeat to a steady rhythm. He slowly moved about, to test his new surroundings. The more he did so, the more he realised that the substance in the tank was actually far less viscous than jelly, lending him a sensation of weightlessness.

'Once the game starts, you'll have five seconds to get your bearings,' Preston continued, 'after that, all hell breaks loose ... and you better be ready. Clear?'

Julius gave him the thumbs up.

'On my mark then – three ... two ... one ... activate!'

The tank began to shake furiously and the now familiar white light, which marked the beginning of a simulation, flooded the space around him.

When Julius was finally able to open his eyes, he found himself staring at a most unexpected sight: he was standing in the middle of a vast green field, under a blue, sunny sky, a warm gentle breeze ruffling his hair.

'What the ...?' he gasped.

He took a few cautious steps forward, all the while trying to assess the situation and check for any signs of danger.

'This must be a combat game,' he said.

Immediately he assumed the combat stance that Professor Chan had taught them in their first Martial Art lesson: his right index and middle finger extended; the other fingers under the thumb. He felt his muscles tensing and his skin tingling. Julius was so absorbed by the sense of that moment that he didn't even notice the tiny electrical discharges sparking off his fingertips.

Up ahead of him was a small forest and he walked towards it, lightly treading on the thick grass. As he entered the shadows of the trees, the air grew still and all went quiet, as if all sound had been sucked into a vacuum. He could see a clearing on the other side and headed in that direction, glancing from side to side as he went. Suddenly, a flock of birds took flight from a nearby tree. Julius froze in his tracks: there was a rumble in the distance, growing ever louder as each second passed, and the ground shook as if a herd of buffaloes was roaring towards him. He staggered backwards and turned to face the source of the noise – instead of buffaloes, a group of at least ten samurai in full armour were hurtling at him. They unsheathed their swords as they ran and let out a battle cry more like the screams of banshees than of humans.

Julius whirled and sprinted towards the clearing, hurdling dead branches and boulders as he went. He was vaguely aware of a small, calmer part of himself that was unconsciously lifting obstacles from his path and flinging them at the chasing pack. In retaliation, a flurry of arrows whistled past his ears. One of them skimmed by inches from his cheek, close enough to fill him with the certainty that he had to get out of the open and find shelter as quickly as possible.

Up ahead he saw a hill crowned by a rocky wall, which looked as good a place as any for him to mount a counterattack. He scampered up to the top where he spun and looked down. The samurai emerged from the line of trees and charged up the hill. At the same time, Julius bent his mind and will into a vision of a roaring fire and, extending his right arm, he unleashed all the energy he could muster. Flames erupted from the ground, lighting the fallen branches and creating a crimson ring at the base of the hill. The samurai skidded to a halt before leaping away from the heat. Julius didn't wait for them to regroup, but instead ran down the other side of the hill. Their screams were still in the air when he was abruptly scooped upward as if by an invisible hand and engulfed by white light. A few seconds later, he found himself on top of the very same hill. Panting, he surveyed the area but there was no trace of the forest or the samurai.

'What next?' he said to no one in particular, wiping sweat from his forehead.

Night was closing in fast and, as darkness crept over the hill, a group of isolated lights appeared in the valley below. Julius, certain that nobody was following him, ran towards them. As he drew nearer, he could hear a faint melody in the air. The source of the music and the lights was a small village. Two rows of wooden houses flanked a dusty main street, which opened out into a square. There was a bonfire at the centre of it, fuelled by thick logs. As Julius walked towards it, he could just about make out the shapes of people dancing on a stage. The delicious smell of popcorn and candy filled his nostrils. He made his way past a burger stall and realised that all the people around him were old and wrinkly, like Mrs Mayflower. When he reached the bonfire, Julius stopped abruptly. What he had mistaken for logs were in fact the scorched bodies of the samurai that had chased him through the forest, their armour piled up to one side.

'No …' he said, stumbling forward.

The music stopped and petrified, Julius watched as the villagers turned to face him. The sweet, plump faces of the old ladies had become grave and sullen, staring at him in eerie silence.

'Stay back!' shouted Julius, even though nobody had moved.

He extended his combat arm in front of him as he backed towards the edge of the square. In unison, the villagers let out a blood-curdling laugh, their mouths agape as they mocked and pointed at him. Julius looked on in horror as their mouths continued to open way beyond human range, so much that their faces were disappearing behind them.

All of a sudden, a voice spoke clearly in his head: *'Don't let them morph. Hit them now!'*

Julius was startled by the voice, but quickly gathered his wits. He bent his mind to the first villager in sight, a haggard old man with alternating teeth, and pushed, sending him flying backward with such force that he took two others with him. Julius switched his attention to three more villagers as they advanced towards him. He lifted one up, just as he had done with Michael back home, and dropped him on top of two ladies. They crashed to the floor and didn't rise again. He had to keep reminding himself that they weren't really old people, but simulated enemies. Several villagers at the back of the group had almost completed their morph. As Julius continued to frantically push people back with his mind, he caught a glimpse of one of them changing, his mouth bent backwards and over his own head. It encircled his body and peeled away, skin and all, revealing a black mass of teeth and hair underneath. The dark shape fell down on all fours, howling with rage.

'You've got to be kidding!' cried Julius. He was exhausted but was still somehow managing to keep the few remaining villagers at bay.

One of the beasts was stalking towards him, its tongue out and its teeth bared in a snarl. Julius knew instantly there was no way he could outrun it. There was only one way out. He backed away from the still morphing villagers and used his remaining strength to bend his mind against the lone beast. He locked his eyes on the creature's and pushed against its mental barriers with all his might, trying to control it. He had never attempted something like this before and, as the pain in his head intensified, he prayed that he would never have to again. The beast kept walking towards him, but its eyes were glazing over and its stride growing heavy. Its head lolled from side to side and, by the time it slumped at Julius's feet, it was utterly defeated.

'Get up!' he ordered with his mind. *'You must carry us to safety!'*

Julius climbed on its back as the beast struggled back up again.

'Come on! Run!' he shouted, seeing that the rest of the villagers had completed their transformation and were closing in on them.

Julius grabbed a clump of its grimy fur and spurred the creature on. They tore through the main street, aiming for the valley that stretched out beyond it. Turning, he saw the pack snapping and snarling at his heels. He aimed his fingers at the closest one, meaning to knock it off course with a shock wave, but managed only to slow it down, as his energy was now almost depleted. One of the beasts caught up with him, so Julius locked his legs around his own creature's chest, threw his hands over the other one and grabbed its ears. He was going to draw from it.

'Share the love, puppy,' he said through gritted teeth.

He felt its energy field pulsing beneath his fingertips and without hesitation took a deep breath and held it. As with his previous

134

draws, he closed his eyes and in his mind's eye saw the blue smoky fluid entering his fingers and his body, replenishing his energy. The beast lost pace dramatically. He was about to release its head when his own ride was knocked down and he was sent crashing to the ground. The last thing he saw were sharp teeth snapping at his flesh as he began to scream. Then the white light enveloped him.

'Hey. Wake up!' Julius heard the voice travelling to him as if from a great distance.

Groggily, he opened his eyes, struggling to remember where he was. Through the liquid haze, he saw Preston's face – he was banging his fist against the tank. As memory flooded back Julius kicked upwards to the surface and grabbed the edge of the tank. Preston jumped onto the platform and joined him there.

'Judging by your state, you must've had one hell of a ride,' said Preston, removing the face shield and helping him out of the tank.

'What happened? How did I do?' asked Julius, checking that his body had not been mutilated by the pack of beasts.

'Dunno kid. The computer is analysing your trip. It will be ready by this evening. Go get changed now.'

Julius was exhausted and felt bruised, even though there were no physical signs that he had been hurt in any way.

'That didn't go too well,' he said to himself as he walked into the shower. He was truly relieved that no one would ever know about his defeat.

RED CAP

Julius decided to go into the courtyard for a moment of rest, but what he found was a quite unexpected sight – Morgana, Faith and Skye were all standing there. Morgana had been crying, judging by her eyes, and the boys were staring at him, speechless.

'What happened?' asked Julius, alarmed. 'Morgana, why are you crying? Is it Kaori?'

'I thought … those beasts had hurt you for real,' she said, sobbing. With that she threw her arms around him and cried some more.

Julius realised then that they must have been watching his Solo game on one of the screens. He stood there in awkward silence, patting Morgana's back until she was ready to let go.

'It was only a game, silly,' said Julius with a smile. 'Sorry I didn't tell you guys, but I couldn't find you and I came here looking for you and then …'

'Man, don't worry. I'm not speechless because of that,' said Skye. 'You were really great!'

'Got killed though,' said Julius, blushing slightly.

'Who cares? That was some hardcore stuff, to be sure!' added Faith excitedly. 'I thought I was watching a horror movie.'

'Yeah, it was brutal,' said Skye.

'I think it's wrong what they turned those lovely old people into,' said Morgana, shaking her head.

'By the way, Skye,' said Julius sheepishly, 'I might have nightmares for a month after tonight. You know, just in case you hear me scream in the middle of the night.'

'I got your back. Come on, let's go for an ice cream. I wanna hear everything.'

Satras was quiet that night. There were only a handful of students doing some last minute shopping and a few other visitors strolling around the lake. Skye had taken them to Mario's Ice-Land, an ice cream parlour on the third level. After furnishing themselves with a matching set of chocolate moustaches, courtesy of Mario's infamous Gut Wrencher Sundae, they all sat back happily as Julius told them about his game. He tried his best to explain how it had felt being chased by the samurai, and the sensation of mentally pushing away the creatures in the village – that had been the really difficult part. He didn't care to admit how scared he had been though or how easy it had been to forget that he was in a simulated combat. Thankfully they didn't ask too many questions on that score, so Julius was able to skirt around it and concentrate instead on the skills he had used.

'Well, mate,' said Faith laying down his spoon, 'you did it. Now we all have to take a shot.'

'Speak for yourself,' said Morgana. 'I'll stick with my flying games for now.'

'I'm with Faith,' said Skye, 'but I'm not telling you when I go either.'

'Speaking of going, we better move. It's almost eight o'clock. I'll get this,' said Morgana, pulling out her wallet.

Julius finished the last of his ice cream and led the way back down. At the Satras station they became quite nervous, as they only had ten minutes left before Foster would lock Tijara's gate.

'Finally, here's the stupid train!' said Faith, hovering above the tracks.

As the train pulled in and drew to a halt, Julius became aware of two men who had queued up ahead of them. Immediately he recognised them as the unpleasant fellows who had been arguing with Pit-Stop Pete on the day of their first game, back in October. Once inside, he leaned against the glass surface of the train and looked over at them. The taller of the two was still wearing the red cap down to his brow and was talking animatedly to the other. The sense of unease that Julius had felt the first time he had seen them was back, stronger than before. There was definitely something not right about them. He decided to do a little mind probing, just for a few seconds, to see if he could pick up any clues as to why he felt so guarded. Locking his eyes on Red Cap, he tried a light mind push. Normally, Julius would have been able to perceive something, but not this time, so he pushed a little harder, but again to no effect. He tried with the other man – same blank.

'That's impossible,' he mumbled.

'What's wrong, Julius?' asked Morgana. She followed his gaze towards the two men.

'Weren't they the ones who upset Pete, back in Satras?' asked Skye.

'The very same. There's something wrong about them. I don't like it,' said Julius, 'and I can't link to either of them.'

The train was now approaching the Zed docks. As it slowed, the men moved towards the door.

'Flaps!' Look there,' whispered Faith, pointing to something outside the train.

They turned to see what had caught Faith's attention and saw a man, crouched by the sensor lock on one of the dock's side doors, unmistakably trying to force it open. Red Cap and his partner had disembarked and were walking straight towards him.

'We've gotta tell someone,' said Morgana, a hint of panic in her voice.

'There's no time,' answered Julius, 'I'm going to stop them.'

'WE are going to stop them,' said Skye emphatically, 'You had your fun with Solo. This is team work. Morgana, go back to Tijara and tell Foster.'

'Hey, I'm in the team too, you know!' she answered resentfully.

'Stop bickering! Let's go before the train leaves. They're already in,' said Julius.

And with that, he darted forward. Faith's skirt hummed behind him, accompanied by the hurried footsteps of Skye and Morgana. Julius stopped outside the door and saw burn marks around the sensor lock. Cautiously, he peered inside and saw the three men walking towards the centre of a large hangar. Motioning for the others to follow, he quietly made his way forward.

The men stopped next to a Cougar where Red Cap uncovered a small green crate by the wall and handed it to one of his accomplices.

'You know what to do,' he said.

His comrade headed towards the end of the hangar at a run. Seeing this, Julius leapt into the light, combat hand at the ready.

'Hey, this area is for Zed members only!' shouted Julius.

Skye, Faith and Morgana came forward and stood by his side. Red Cap turned to face them, a dangerous smirk on his face.

'Hmph, it's the granny-killer,' he scoffed.

Julius barely had time to register what he had just been called before Red Cap whipped something from his pocket and threw it at the Cougar next to him. There was a small explosion that blew one of its wings off and dark smoke billowed out into the hangar. Julius covered his face just in time to protect himself from metal fragments that were flying through the air. Through the smoke, he was relieved to see that Faith had shielded Morgana with his skirt. He ran towards Red Cap with Faith in tow while Skye and Morgana went for the other man, who was trying to hide behind the crippled plane.

Julius tried to push Red Cap off balance, by hitting him with a volley of short energy bursts, but to his dismay they weren't inflicting any damage. His shockwaves rippled through the air, passed harmlessly through Red Cap and dispersed against the far wall. Faith's efforts were also in vain. Either they had both suddenly lost their mind-skills or this guy was protected by some invisible shield.

Red Cap let out a spiteful laugh and threw another bomb at them. Luckily Faith had seen it coming and with remarkably quick reflexes flew straight at Julius, lifted him off his feet and dived for the safety of a nearby column. The device exploded just behind them, sending them flying. They landed hard and Julius sprang to his feet just in time to see Red Cap disappearing through the back door of the hangar.

Julius turned to his right and saw that Morgana and Skye were still fighting against the last of their enemy, who just stood there, motionless. Their attacks were proving as ineffective as his had been. He sprinted forward and, for no logical reason, scrambled onto a crate and dived at the man. But, as Julius closed his arms around his neck, he grasped nothing but fresh air and ended up sprawled across the floor. As he landed with a thud, a bright red light lit up the room for a second and blinked out just as quickly. Then all was still.

'Julius, are you OK man?' asked Skye, helping him up.

'Yeah, I'm fine ... I think. Where's that guy gone?'

'He just ... vanished,' said Morgana, struggling to catch her breath.

'Not before dropping this,' said Faith, holding up a small red box. 'It fell off as you passed through him.'

'What's that?' asked Skye, shaking some dust from his hair.

'No idea. Maybe ...' Faith was cut short by the sound of feet running toward them.

Captain Foster had just entered the hangar, closely followed by ten security guards. He stood there flabbergasted, looking from the four dusty students to the crippled Cougar leaning on its one remaining wing. After a few seconds, he seemed to regain some composure and turned to his men.

'Alert the Grand Master that there's been a security breach in the Zed docks. I shall be along shortly with the students. And send a repair team to the hangar, pronto!'

Julius looked at the others anxiously. How they were going to explain this to Freja was anybody's guess, and judging by Foster's stern expression, he was sure they were in big trouble.

Twenty minutes later, they were all standing to attention in Cress's office, their uniforms singed from the explosions and greyed by the dust. Julius's eyes kept flicking towards Freja, who was sitting silently behind Cress's desk. He was staring at the red box in his hands, his eyes focused and grave. Julius felt positively petrified – being in the presence of the Grand Master was intimidating enough as it was without the added burden of this unpleasant incident. Master Cress, who was standing by Freja's side, listened into his earpiece for a few moments before addressing the students: 'I believe an explanation is in order. Mr Miller?'

Skye began to talk. He told how they had seen the men arguing with Pete back in October and then noticed them again on the train. To Julius's surprise, Skye made no mention of his failed mind-linking attempts and skipped straight to how Faith had seen them breaking into the hangar and everything that had followed.

'But, instead of alerting security from aboard the Intra-Rail System,' said Cress seriously, 'you decided to take it upon yourselves to eliminate the threat. Who may we thank for the partial destruction of the hangar, the Cougar and the possible death of four Tijara students?'

'It was me, sir,' said Julius quickly, 'I am the one responsible.'

'This isn't the Hologram Palace, Mr McCoy. Leave heroic stunts for your Solo games. In real life, you belong to Zed and we act as a collective.'

Julius felt his cheeks burning with shame but somehow managed to keep his eyes fixed on the Master.

Cress stared at them in silence for several excruciating seconds.

'You are all banned from Satras until the mid-winter break. From tomorrow, for the next three weeks, between 17:00 and 20:00 hours, you shall report daily to Professor Chan for extra Martial Arts lessons. You are under direct order not to mention any of today's events to anybody ... and that includes the red box. Understood?'

'Yes sir,' they answered promptly.

'Report to Dr Walliser in the infirmary. Dismissed.'

They bowed low and left the room. Once in the corridor, Julius stopped and quietly pressed his ear against the closed door.

'Are you crazy?' whispered Skye.

Julius hushed him and gestured for the others to join him. He could see they were all anxious, but their sense of curiosity was obviously stronger than their fear because they moved closer without hesitation.

'Nathan,' Freja's slightly muffled voice said, 'retrieve the footage from the dock's surveillance cameras. I want exterior and interior views. And have List examine this box immediately.'

'Do you think it's ...'

'Salgoria. Who else?'

Julius stiffened at the mention of the Queen of Arnesh. There was a sharp intake of breath behind him – probably Morgana. He heard steps approaching the door, so brusquely he pushed the others along the corridor until they were clear of the office block. Nobody said anything but, judging by their expressions, Julius knew they were as worried as he was. The idea that Salgoria's men had infiltrated Zed right under their noses was scarier than any detention.

In the infirmary, the nurses took them all into separate rooms. Dr Walliser disinfected a few cuts and bruises on Julius's arms and face and then released him. He made his way to the mess hall where he was going to meet the others for some food, a chat about what they had just heard and perhaps a little rant about what seemed like an undeserved detention. But, as he approached, he heard raucous laughter and chanting, as if someone was having a huge party. Curious, he stepped into the room and, before he had time to understand what was going on, the cheering doubled in volume and he was instantly surrounded by his entire year. Hands pulled at him from all directions – a sea of laughing faces danced in front of him as his classmates patted him on the back and heartily congratulated him. Julius was totally mystified by the situation and it wasn't until he saw Skye bouncing merrily on one of the benches, pointing at the Solo screen, that he realised what was going on. He looked up and saw his own name on the ninth rank of the board. A beautiful smile lit up his face and, as he pushed his way towards Skye, he was positively beaming.

'Paint me green and call me a leprechaun. You did it!' shouted Faith, gliding over the tables.

Skye leapt from the table and landed in Julius's arms hooting, while Morgana clapped and cheered with Siena. Julius shook hands with most of the students in the mess hall, answered questions and vaguely dodged a few of the older girls who were trying to hug him. Thankfully Morgana came to the rescue, announcing, businesslike, to the crowd that his food was getting cold. When Julius went to bed that night, he was still grinning, the fear of Salgoria forgotten for a while.

The three weeks before the mid-winter break went by quicker than Julius could have anticipated. The news of his Solo score had spread like wildfire. Someone had apparently made an illegal copy of the footage from his game and circulated it among the three schools. Kaori had reported that his game was the most viewed inside the Palace arena, which made Julius mighty pleased with himself. During his breaks, he was often surrounded by small crowds eager to hear all about the morphing grannies and the skills he had used.

Not once had his friends complained about their detention,

which Julius thought was only fair and decent of them given that, although he had been the one to start the chase in the hangars, he had not obliged them to follow. They had made their choice and were paying the consequences just as he was.

With all the extra Martial Arts training, they were getting fitter and stronger, which made a big difference in their regular classes. Banned as they were from Satras, their only chance of getting anywhere near a plane's cockpit was during their Pilot Training on Fridays, and they enjoyed the lessons all the more for it. Spaceology was still rather boring for most of the students in comparison to the other subjects, except for Morgana of course. On the last Wednesday morning before the holidays, after being hit on her head for the umpteenth time by an eraser, courtesy of Skye, she stood up and stopped Professor Brown.

'Excuse me, Professor,' she said throwing an evil glance at Skye, 'I can't quite hear you from here. Shall I move to a closer desk?'

Professor Brown looked a little puzzled, especially after seeing three of her students stifling a laugh.

'Of course, Miss Ruthier. Take a seat. Now, as I was saying,' she continued, 'Kratos is an artificial disc, built by Zed around fifty years ago. Its purpose was that of a storage facility for the Academy. However, it has never been utilised due to its gravitational instability whenever a solar flare occurs. It is very close to our sector and its atmosphere is breathable thanks to a shield, much like Zed's. However ...'

The bell cut her short and she dismissed the class with a frustrated expression, given that most of the students were already at the door. But, while Professor Brown had seemed oblivious of the holiday spirit among the students, Professor King, the Telekinesis teacher, had embraced it a little too enthusiastically. The following morning, Julius's class was divided into two groups for a massive mental tug-of-war session. Professor King, sporting a Santa Claus hat, was instructing them from the back of an embalmed reindeer called Jeff, which was gliding along the classroom under his telekinetic guidance.

'Show off,' said Faith under his breath.

'I want the teams in two rows facing each other, two yards away from the white line. Once in position, you must hold hands. On my signal, you shall try to bring the other team towards you and over the line. Since it's your first time I would advise you to concentrate on the student directly opposite you.'

King stopped his steed between the teams.

'Ho, ho, ho! Ready...steady...go!'

Julius felt a sudden tugging sensation in his chest, which pulled him forward slightly. He regained his footing and concentrated on Skye, who was standing opposite him. Pulling with his mind was harder than he had thought and it felt very weird indeed. Holding hands with fourteen other people meant that his efforts were being spread right across the line. He felt like an electric conductor, with the energy of his team mates passing through his body. Professor King was laughing his head off, which didn't help Julius's concentration at all.

'If you could see yourselves! Here, let me take a picture,' he said, laughing even harder, while pulling a camera out of his pocket.

Julius could only imagine why. The class was totally silent, without the shouting and the cheering that would normally accompany an activity such as this. All any spectator would see was thirty people grunting in concentration, their faces red and their brows dangerously close to their mouths. Julius forced these thoughts out of his mind and focused instead on Skye. He could see the other team advancing unevenly towards the line, which allowed him to see who was pulling the hardest. Morgana, who was holding his left hand, started to slide forward too, thanks to the efforts of Yuri Slovich. Julius redoubled his pull, and after several painful minutes, the other team began to slip forward faster and faster. Skye, who was holding his ground stoically, was forced across the line by the people to either side of him. The first cry in the room came from Barth, who literally flew over the line compliments of Faith.

'I think I've ruptured a blood vessel,' said Skye, rubbing his forehead.

Professor King was spurring his dead steed across the room, dismissing the class with one final "Ho, ho, ho!".

'He needs a holiday more than we do ...' whispered Morgana as they left.

OF PARTIES AND JUNKYARDS

The last day of term came and went and, by dinner time, Julius was as happy as he could be. He had finally managed his first brief trance, during that morning's session with Master Isshin.

'I'm so glad for you, Julius,' said Morgana, nimbly picking at her vegetable tempura with a pair of chopsticks. 'I knew you could do it.'

'What did the holopal do – hit you over the head with a hammer?' asked Skye with a grin.

'He was tempted, but no. I was actually considering giving up, thinking that I would try again after the holiday, when all of a sudden I just zoned out. I think I was so relaxed about it that it just happened by itself.'

'Was Master Isshin pleased?' asked Morgana.

'Yes ... for about two seconds. Then he flickered and disappeared on me again. I bet there's something wrong with this watch. Maybe I've damaged it or something.'

'Who cares,' said Skye. 'Now that you've done it, Cress will be satisfied and you'll be able to sleep again in the morning.'

'I hope so, oh so much.'

And, sure enough, when he returned to his quarters Julius found his computer monitor beeping – there was a message from Gabriel List asking him to return the watch in the morning, as he wouldn't need it anymore. With deep satisfaction, he deactivated his alarm clock and buried himself under the blanket.

It was close to midday by the time Julius dragged himself out of bed and headed for the holographic sector. He knocked on the technicians' door, while undoing the strap of his watch.

'Mr McCoy,' said List after opening the door, 'I see you got my message. Come inside.'

Upon entering, Gabriel dropped all formalities, as he had done before. He invited Julius to sit, shoved a cup of hot chocolate into his hands and asked about his experiences with the holopal. As Julius recounted the details of his sessions, List became ever more animated. It reminded him incredibly of how excited Faith got whenever he talked about anything to do with the latest gadgets and gizmos, and he made a mental note to introduce the pair of them at the earliest opportunity.

'I am glad Master Isshin was able to help,' said List, sipping from his cup.

'You're telling me. By the way, you might need to check the program.'

'You mean it disappeared on you again?'

'Yes, just after my trance. Maybe the excitement was too much and he blew a circuit, or something.'

'It is possible,' said List, half smiling, 'except it's not the first watch that's packed up on us this month. I better go check the VI core. Anyway, if you should need Master Isshin again, you know where to find him.'

Julius thanked him and headed to the mess hall, where he grabbed some food and took it with him to the garden. Morgana, Faith and Skye were lying on the grass. Skye waved as he approached.

'About time,' he said, making space beside him.

'Thanks for letting me sleep this morning,' said Julius.

'I figured you'd kill me if I didn't.'

'Too true. So what's up?'

'At breakfast, they gave us the schedule for our mid-winter family meals,' said Skye. 'And here's the really cool bit – we get to have them in the Hologram Palace.'

'Yeah,' said Morgana, sitting up, 'we can program in any setting we want! The slot for our year is on the 28th.'

'Sounds good,' said Julius.

'Not really,' said Faith gloomily, ''cause it means that the Palace will be off limits from now until New Year.'

'Shoot,' said Julius, disappointed. 'My little brother will be gutted.'

'I know,' said Morgana. 'But at least Michael will have a meal in there. Why don't you let him choose the program, Julius?'

'Good idea. He'll like that. What are you guys going for?'

'Well,' said Skye, 'all of the Terra 3 people have a meal together every year. Apparently, it's a tradition as old as the Zed space stations.'

'Who else is from Terra 3 in our year?' asked Julius.

'Louisa Call, Yuri Slovich, Annette Valeris and Morgana's friend, Isolde Frey. I grew up with them. I mean, there are only so many places you can go to when you're on a space station. But hey, it's home,' said Skye with a shrug of his shoulders. 'What about you, Faith?'

'I thought of going somewhere in the Hawaiian Archipelagos. You know, sun, sand and surf. Besides, me Ma' loves to sunbathe.'

'That sounds better than my party,' said Skye. 'You don't mind if I barge in, do you?'

'To be sure.'

'We're going to have our usual traditional Japanese meal,' said Morgana. 'My mum bought us all new kimonos when she visited Kyoto last month. I think she got one for you too, Julius,' she said, turning towards him.

'Excellent! I'm looking forward to seeing her.'

'You guys been friends long?' asked Skye.

'Morgana is practically my sister,' said Julius, trying to steal one of the dried apricots she was snacking on.

'I prefer to think of myself as his good conscience,' she said, quickly moving the food out of reach. 'We grew up on the same street, went to the same school and all the rest. So you *could* say we're like family.' As she said that, she lightly ran her fingers through his hair and ruffled them.

Julius took his chance and lunged at the apricots, grabbing a handful as he rolled across the grass before leaping up triumphantly. 'Thank you. Thank you very much. I'm here all week,' he said, bowing to an invisible crowd. 'I'm off to speak to Michael. See you later guys.'

Morgana waved him away with a mock expression of frustration and, lying back, resumed reading her book. As Julius was about to turn away, he caught Skye looking at her and noticed a light pink wisp above his head. He turned the other way, suddenly very embarrassed.

'I really don't need to know,' he muttered to himself as he hastily left the garden.

It took about two hours of messaging back and forth before

Michael finally decided what program he wanted for the holiday meal. With this information, Julius went to Satras to book a slot. Mrs Mayflower was all smiles and praise for his Solo score when she saw him and Julius, who was surrounded by several queuing students, blushed nervously and wished she would just get on with it. It was bad enough that Bernard Docherty was staring at him from the sidelines – Julius thought he resented him for making it onto the score board – but it got worse when he placed his order for the holosuite. For reasons unknown to Julius, Michael had decided to have the meal in the middle of a junkyard.

'Do you want a tetanus shot with that?' Mrs Mayflower asked with a concerned look.

Their parents had tried to dissuade Michael in every way and with numerous bribes, but he had not budged.

'A junkyard?' asked Faith over his tea that night.

'Has he gone mad?' said Morgana.

'Suddenly my shindig with the colonists sounds like fun,' added Skye, with a perplexed look on his face.

'Faith, I forbid you to mention Hawaii to me until the end of the year,' said Julius, brandishing a turkey leg at him.

'I'll try mate,' said Faith, seriously. 'So, you gonna eat *junk* food?'

The four of them looked at each other and burst out laughing, while Julius pelted Faith with turkey bones.

The following week Satras was packed with visitors, day and night. Each student's family was allowed to stay only for 24 hours, to avoid overcrowding. With the Hologram Palace closed, Julius and his mates spent most of their days walking around Satras, catching up with other classmates, visiting Mario's Ice-Land and exploring the many shops scattered across the various levels.

On the morning of the 28th, Julius went to pick his family up from the docks. As he waited for their shuttle, his mind turned to the fight with Red Cap and his men. Cress had not mentioned the incident even once, as if he wanted them to forget all about it. As far as he knew, it had remained a secret from the rest of Zed too. It wasn't as if Julius thought about it constantly, but it was hard to forget that he had been involved in a serious incident like that – the memories were there, stored in the back of his head.

'Julius!' cried Michael, jumping off the shuttle and running wildly towards his brother.

Julius caught him in his arms and squeezed him. Jenny and Rory McCoy followed their youngest son a little more elegantly, although Julius could see his dad's eyes keenly scanning the area. After several minutes of hugs, kisses and more hugs – Hasn't our son grown so much, Rory? – Julius led them aboard the Intra-Rail System that would take them to their hotel in Satras.

Julius couldn't help but smile as he watched them soaking in the new surroundings with sheer delight on their faces. It strongly reminded him of his own excitement when he had first seen Zed. Satras surely was a mighty sight for them and one day was not nearly enough to enjoy all of its amusements. After checking in they set off for their meal, deciding that they would do some exploring later.

As they reached the Palace, they were directed by security guards to use the left door and to go two floors down. Julius explained to Michael that this was the same entrance he used for the games. His brother was looking everywhere and touching everything, overjoyed to be there at last. When they reached their floor, they stopped behind Dhara Sundaram, an Indian girl in his year. Julius watched as Dhara and her family stepped onto a lift. Its metal doors closed as soon as they were in and slid away before disappearing behind the wall to their left, before being promptly replaced by a new lift. Julius, who had read the instructions several times that morning, walked confidently towards it. He cleared his throat and gave the command: 'Computer, activate 1MJ McCoy.'

Julius invited his family to enter the lift and as they stepped inside, the door shut behind them and the floor began to move. When the lift stopped, another door opened revealing the biggest junkyard the McCoys had ever seen.

Even with all of his holographic experience, Julius was blown away. The junkyard seemed to spread out forever in pile upon pile of trash of every kind. Tiny fairy lights gave a festive glow to the drabness of the place, creating fantastic shadows all around. At the centre of an empty area, they saw a table laden with an impossible amount of food and drinks. The table itself was sculpted from the oddest pieces of junk compressed together. Julius could distinguish a fridge door, a fly-car seat and even a teddy bear. The backs of the chairs curled upwards, creating tall, elegant metal frames.

'Shall we?' said Rory, inviting his family to sit down.

'Is it safe to eat this food, Julius?' asked Jenny anxiously.

'Of course it is, dear,' cut in Rory, 'perfectly safe. Michael and I were so excited about coming here that we looked it up, didn't we son?'

Michael nodded his agreement, but his mouth was already too crammed with food to add any comment. As they began their meal, Rory explained to his wife how the holosuite was programmed to convert energy to matter and back again, which allowed them to physically interact with their surroundings.

'The food you're eating darling, is the same as you would get on a spaceship. It's replicated through a protein re-sequencer ...'

At that point Julius had to stifle a laugh, as he realised that his mum couldn't understand half of what Mr McCoy was saying.

'Dad, I think you've confused her enough,' said Julius, helping himself to a large portion of mash.

'Maybe you're right, son. Why don't you tell us about you now?' said Rory jovially.

Julius was glad to finally be able to speak to them in person about his new life. Writing or talking through a sat-cam wasn't really the same. He had always spoken to his parents about everything, knowing that they would listen and try to understand, no matter what he was going through. But, as he told them about his friends, his success in the game world and his failure in Meditation, it dawned on him that he wasn't going to be able to tell them about his fight in the docks. He had been ordered not to mention it to anyone and, being a Zed student, he had to follow the rules. Knowing that, however, didn't make it any easier to keep it from his parents.

When he had finished, Jenny shared the news from home, which Julius was eager to hear. After lunch, Michael spent a good hour rummaging in the piles of junk, assembling the weirdest gadgets and toys. It broke his heart, but Julius had to tell his brother that, once out of the holosuite, all his possessions would disappear.

'I know,' said Michael sadly. 'It's the matter-energy conversion. I've looked it up.'

'I'm impressed. What say we go shopping for some real gadgets in Satras?'

'Excellent. Let's go!' said Michael, rushing everyone off their seats.

'That's a good idea,' said Jenny. 'I think I've had enough of the junkyard. Besides, I want to try and find some lunar memorabilia for your granny.'

They spent the rest of the afternoon walking around Satras and, in the evening, went to Mario's to meet up with Morgana, Kaori and their parents. Julius was beaming when Mrs Ruthier gave him his kimono, and Michael begged her to bring one back for him the next time she was in Japan.

'I'll save the money. I promise,' he said sincerely.

They stayed up quite late but, even with their parents there, Julius and Morgana had to return to Tijara by midnight. The morning after, the two families caught the shuttle back to Earth together, leaving Julius, Morgana and Kaori waving goodbye to them from the platform.

'That was fun,' said Morgana, watching the shuttle take off. 'Too bad it was only one day.'

'We'll see them soon enough Hana-chan,' said Kaori, putting an arm around Morgana's shoulders as they boarded the train back to the schools. 'Besides, we still have two exciting events coming up – the New Year party and your birthday.'

'Too right. I'm so looking forward to it!'

'How does the party work?' asked Julius.

'Each school has their own one, normally in the assembly hall.'

'Oh,' said Morgana, clearly disappointed. 'I thought that we'd be together.'

'I know,' said Kaori, 'I would have liked that too. There are so few events that get all three schools together, like the ceremony for a new Grand Master for example. But I'll see you during the day and I'm sure you'll have a great time at the party, even without your big sister. You'll take care of that, won't you Julius?'

'Sure thing. And we've even prepared a little surprise for you.'
Morgana smiled and clapped her hands together excitedly.
'See? All sorted, sis.'

The train slowed down and stopped at Tijara, so they said goodbye to Kaori and went in search of their friends.

On the afternoon of New Year's Eve, Julius's dorm was in a state of total panic. Apparently not one of the first years was able to make an acceptable bowtie and in the end they unanimously decided that Lopaka Liway would fetch Tony Tower and bring him there, by force if necessary. To their relief, Tower arrived along with three of his mates, and they happily went from room to room making sure that all the young students looked impeccable.

Julius and Skye were standing in front of the mirror, meticulously smoothing the creases from their jackets. For the New Year party, all students had to wear a black, tailored dinner suit, with white shirt and black tie. Julius had collected his own after lunch, from Twitch and Stitch, the schools' uniform supplier in Satras.

'Don't we look just!' said Skye, combing his hair.

'Just,' said Julius feeling rather anxious. He was always self-conscious at these kinds of formal events and was hoping to find a table in the darkest corner of the room.

'Are you guys ready?' asked Faith, knocking on the door.

'Come in,' said Skye with one last futile attempt to flatten his wavy hair.

Faith glided into the room, his metallic skirt as black as his jacket.

'How did you do that?' asked Julius, surprised.

'It was Pete. He left a tub of dark polish at Twitch and Stitch, in case I felt like … coordinating!'

'Just watch you don't get too close to any of the girls' dresses,' said Skye.

'Oh, no worries. It's already dry. Anyway, I doubt anybody would ask me to dance.'

'We'll dance with you, Faith,' said Skye with a wink.

'Speak for yourself,' said Julius, pushing them both out of the room.

They made their way up to the hall, checking that their bowties were still facing the right direction. As he stepped out of the lift, Julius was startled by the large crowd in the main corridor. There were 180 Mizki students in Tijara, and tonight they would all be gathered in the same place. They were huddled in small groups, some sitting by the fountain that ran around the black walls of the assembly room, and others just milling about. Everyone looked exceptionally smart and very official, but Julius could tell there was a sense of anxious anticipation in the air. He didn't even need to concentrate to see the little wisps of pink rising above the heads of the senior boys as they discreetly ogled the girls mingling in the crowd.

'Hey guys,' said Morgana from behind them.

Julius turned and saw her and Siena approaching them.

'Ladies, you look wonderful,' said Faith, bowing ceremoniously.

'Thank you,' they both answered, blushing.

Julius also thought that they looked really pretty, but he most definitely wasn't going to share that thought with them. Morgana was wearing a long, strapless, emerald green satin dress. The folds of the gown made Julius think of soft tropical waves, draping smoothly towards the ground. On her shoulder, she wore a velvet stole of the same colour.

'Happy birthday, Morgana,' Julius said cheerfully. Then he sent a quick mind message to Skye, who was staring at the girls with the glazed expression of a sloth.

'*Close your mouth, you ape!*'

Skye was startled out of his reverie, but managed to recompose himself without the girls noticing.

At that moment, the doors of the assembly hall opened and the students started to file in. When Julius entered the hall, his eyes wandered up to the ceiling. The roof panels had been slid open, allowing them to see the bright stars beyond the Zed shield. The room looked different from their first visit. All the chairs had been replaced by circular tables, covered with white linen and silver candleholders. The flickering lights created intimate glows and cast shadows all around. The tables formed a semi-circle facing the stage, where a long table had been prepared for the teachers.

'There's a free table over there,' said Morgana, pointing to her left.

They hurried in that direction and Julius headed straight for the most hidden of the chairs. That left three empty seats, which were soon taken by Lopaka, Isolde and her roommate Femi Mubarak, a girl from Egypt. Waiters in white uniforms moved swiftly from table to table, bringing filled champagne flutes to all the Mizki. Watching them dodge the students with remarkable agility, Julius thought about the first and only time he had tasted champagne, at his parents' wedding anniversary, but he couldn't remember whether he had liked it or not.

As the last of the students found their seats, Master Cress entered the hall. He walked over to the stage and faced the Mizki.

'All rise,' he said aloud, lifting his hands upwards.

The students rose quickly to their feet and the noise died down.

Julius followed Cress's gaze toward the main door, where the Grand Master of Tijara was standing, impeccably dressed. Freja stepped into the room followed by the teachers, all wearing black – even Chan and Lao-tzu had swapped their usual tunics for dark suits. They walked to their table and stood behind their chairs.

'Please, be seated,' Freja said to all.

Julius sat down, trying to shake off the shameful memory of his last meeting with him.

'It is with great honour that I welcome you all to this special event,' said Freja, bowing his head to the assembly. 'Two hundred and thirty-five years ago, Marcus Tijara stood on this very stage, addressing the first ever Mizki students. Much time has passed since then, but his dream of building a peaceful society has never died and it continues to shape Zed's ethos, even today. I would like you to raise your glasses with me, to the teachers and staff of Tijara, for their constant contribution to that dream.'

Freja and the Mizki raised their glasses together to the teachers, who were bowing to them in return.

'Tonight,' continued Freja, 'we celebrate the end of another year spent in peace and prosperity. May the year 2856 be as peaceful and prosperous.'

'So let it be,' answered the assembly in unison.

Freja took his seat and the waiters began to serve dinner. As the evening progressed, Julius felt his anxiety ebbing away and sensed that this night would be a fine one. He was having a mighty good time with his mates; the food was excellent and his ego had been suitably boosted, as several Mizki Seniors had made their way over to the table to congratulate him personally on his Solo score. After dessert, fifteen couples, made up entirely of 6 Mizki Seniors, moved to the empty floor and opened the dances to the notes of Strauss's waltz.

'My sister told me it's a tradition for the final year students to open the dances,' Morgana told her girlfriends with an excited giggle.

'They look so beautiful,' said Siena dreamily.

Given that the girls were all busy watching the dancers, Julius decided it was the perfect moment to bring out Morgana's surprise. He had arranged everything with the chef that very afternoon and, with a nod of his head, he signalled to the waiter that they were ready. As the last notes of the music faded away, a beautiful birthday cake made its way to their table. Morgana's eyes grew wide and bright when she saw it, and so great was her joy that she remained speechless. The table started to sing "Happy Birthday" not so loud as to attract the attention of the entire room, but enough so that the adjacent tables joined in.

'Thank you, guys,' said Morgana tearfully. 'Thank you so much.'

'Come on, make a wish,' said Skye with a big smile.

Morgana closed her eyes for few seconds, then blew out the candles in one go, all thirteen of them. Julius started to clap and everybody else joined in with loud cheers. He knew that Morgana had been well and truly pleased with the surprise because, as she looked at him, he could see a bright aura spreading all around her head and shoulders like a glittering cape.

'I wish they could see that,' thought Julius with a smile. In his mind that was the best thank you, better than any words she could have said.

As midnight drew near, Julius watched the students dancing wildly all around the room. It seemed that the dance floor was too small for all of them. Morgana and Isolde were also in the crowd, with Faith doing a mad hover-dance between them.

'I hope that skirt holds him up,' said Julius with a grin.

'Come on. Let's go and make sure it does,' said Skye, dragging him to the dance floor.

With ten seconds left before the bells, the DJ began the countdown and everyone joined in. As the clock struck midnight the hall erupted in joyful cheers, while a formation of Zed's Cougars flew across the sky. Their sharp turns and twists generated a huge roar from the crowd and they all clapped wildly.

'Happy Hogmanay, Julius,' said Morgana hugging him tightly.

'To our first space party,' said Faith, spinning out of control above their heads.

The music started again for a celebration that would continue into the small hours of the night.

Around one o'clock, Julius and Faith left Morgana and Skye on the dance floor, to make a quick visit to the restroom behind the main stage. Suddenly, as they were coming out again, Faith grabbed Julius by the arm and pushed him behind a thick curtain.

'What the ...' started Julius.

Faith clamped his hand over Julius's mouth and pointed to his left where Freja and Cress were standing, engrossed in what appeared to be an intense discussion. Julius moved quietly towards them and peeked out of a gap in the curtains. Although they were keeping their voices low, Julius and Faith could hear them well enough.

'Are you sure, Nathan?' asked Freja. His voice sounded worried and tense.

'Positive. Salgoria's troops have occupied Kratos. We just don't know why.'

'What about the red box?'

'That's the worst news of all. It's a hologram remote control, with the added power of a scrambler. It's very advanced technology. Salgoria is a proper Arneshian. But ... you don't seem surprised, Carlos.'

'I've examined the CCTV footage from the hangar. The scan analysis has revealed two distinct electromagnetic interferences.'

'McCoy and his friends were telling the truth then.'

'Yes, but we never doubted that. In the meantime, order a scan of all holographic devices on Zed. List said he's been having some problems recently.'

Julius froze as he remembered the numerous times when Master Isshin had flickered and vanished during their meditation training.

'Are they here for him, Marcus?'

'Yes. Somehow they've found out.'

'I'll have him followed then.'

'Do it. We cannot risk another Bastiaan Grant. Not this time. And especially not with him.'

'Anything else?'

'That will be all for now, Nathan.'

As they walked away, Julius and Faith moved back towards the restroom.

'We've gotta tell the others,' said Julius seriously. 'Let's go.'

Ten minutes later, they were all sitting in the garden, the cheerfulness gone from their faces.

'I can't believe we fought against holograms,' said Skye, shaking his head.

'It makes sense,' answered Julius. 'All our mind-skills went right through them.'

'And when you knocked the device from that thing's head, it just disappeared,' added Faith.

'They were using the holonet,' said Julius, 'that's why Master Isshin wasn't working properly and why Red Cap called me a "granny-killer" – he was in the net. He knew exactly what I was doing in that Solo game.'

'Given that it worked as a scrambler, it's no wonder you couldn't read their minds, Julius, not in Satras and not in the train,' said Morgana.

'What were they doing here, anyway?' asked Skye. 'Testing that remote device?'

'I think they were doing more than that,' said Julius. 'Freja mentioned Bastiaan Grant. You know what that means.'

'Wasn't he the Tuala Master that disappeared a few years back?' asked Morgana. 'Kaori told me about it.'

'They think the Arneshians are here to kidnap someone else?' asked Skye.

'Yes. And they seem to know who he is, because Freja has asked to have him followed.'

'Right,' said Faith, 'but what about the hologram that ran away with that box? Where did it go? Is their ship still at Pete's dock? And why are the Arneshians occupying Kratos?'

'Remember what Professor Brown said before the winter break?' said Morgana. 'She told us that Kratos is an empty man-made disc and that it's very close to our sector.'

'Then it's no coincidence, whatever their reasons are,' said Faith.

They discussed the matter further but still couldn't find answers to the many questions. To avoid suspicion they returned to the party, the thought of dancing completely gone from their minds.

They continued to discuss the news until two o'clock, when the last song faded away and the students were asked to retire for the night.

As he lay in bed, in the darkness, Julius felt the threat of Salgoria creeping over him.

'What a way to end the year,' he said to Skye.

'Amen to that.'

FLIGHT TIME

With the mid-winter break over, life in the school returned to normal. On their first Monday back, Julius attended his Meditation lesson without the usual dread and sure enough he managed to slip into a trance within the set target of a minute. Although Morgana was still the quickest in their year – thirty seconds – Julius was at least even with Skye and Faith, which gave Professor Lao-tzu reason to congratulate him on his achievement.

After lunch, they walked to the holographic sector for their Telekinesis lesson. As they entered, Professor King asked them to sit.

'It is customary at this time of year to introduce the 1 Mizki Juniors to the Spring Missions,' he said.

At that announcement the silence was interrupted by a buzz of excited whispers.

'As you may know,' continued King, 'the curriculum for the two junior years is the same for all students. In third year, on the other hand, you will be able to choose specialised subjects. The Spring Missions and the Summer Camps are opportunities for you to sample the different paths available to Zed graduates.'

'Guess where I'm going,' whispered Morgana eagerly to Julius.

'However, there has been a change of plans,' continued Professor King seriously.

The class fell silent again. Julius threw a glance at Faith, and received an equally worried look in return.

'From this year, the school will be deciding the nature of your first mission. It has been agreed that all Mizki Juniors will spend two weeks on the Earth colonies. More details will be given in due course.'

Some of the students seemed excited by that prospect, but others weren't quite sure what to think about the change, judging by their perplexed faces. Julius, however, had more than a clear idea of why this was happening, and he wasn't the only one.

'We should have seen it coming,' said Morgana once the lesson was over.

They were walking back to the lounge to finish an essay on ship catalysts for Professor Clavel, which was due by the end of the week.

'They're sending all MJ's as far away as possible from any action,' said Julius, annoyed.

'If anything happens,' said Morgana, 'the Arneshians will have to pass through Zed and its colonies before they get to us. I guess it's understandable that they want us out of the way. Shame though, I was really looking forward to some real flight training.'

'It's not fair. We're probably the only four students in the whole of Zed with any idea of what's going on and they don't even bother asking us if we want to do our part,' continued Julius animatedly. 'I mean, we actually fought against Salgoria's men ... things!'

'Speaking of four,' said Skye looking around, 'where's Shanigan got to?'

'I don't know. He was behind us when we left class,' said Morgana, checking the lounge. 'Anyway, let's not talk in here. Remember we're under orders not to discuss the situation with anybody. I don't want to get into any more trouble if I can help it.'

Julius nodded in agreement, but he was still frustrated. It wasn't so much that he couldn't choose his mission – after all, visiting the regular colonies was a great experience – the truth was that the fight in the hangar had left him craving more action. That, and the fact that Red Cap had mocked and defeated him. If he had shared any of these feelings with the others, they would surely have told him to let it go; that he couldn't have known they were holograms; he had only just started training and he was lucky to be alive. Julius knew all of this already. Perhaps it simply boiled down to the fact that he hated losing and Red Cap reminded him all too much of people like Billy Somers – the sneering, taunting characters who loved to make others feel useless. It seemed unfair that, as soon as Somers had been put in his place by his own bravado and disappeared from the scene, Red Cap had come along to cause a whole new set of problems.

Four hours later, Julius, Skye and Morgana were sitting in the mess hall, having their dinner. Skye was swallowing freshly made ravioli like there was no tomorrow.

'Good grief, boy!' said Morgana looking at him, her face caught somewhere between disgust and amazement. 'Why don't you eat space and time while you're at it?'

'That's not a mouth,' added Julius, 'it's a black hole.'

'But I'm hungry!' said Skye shrugging his shoulders. 'Anyway, still no sign of Faith. I bet you a Fyver he's gone to try out Solo.'

'And you would lose that bet,' answered Faith, patting him on the shoulder.

168

'Where did you go?' asked Morgana, moving her bag from the chair so Faith could sit next to her.

'I paid a visit to Mr Pete,' said Faith with an enigmatic smile.

'Well?' asked Julius. 'What did you find out?'

'After class I went to Satras. Pete has a shop on the second tier. They sell tools and spare parts and the like. He's rarely there, but the attendant can contact him. So I told him who I was and made an excuse that I needed to see him.'

'What excuse?' asked Julius suspiciously.

'I tore off a panel from the back of me skirt actually.'

'You're a maniac!' said Skye giving him the thumbs up.

'And it worked. Pete came to see me and fixed it, no problem. As he was working, I took the liberty of asking a few questions ... the right questions might I add. When I mentioned those guys, he went mental. He said they'd disappeared and nobody had come to collect those boxes they left behind, but they too mysteriously disappeared one day. And on New Year's Eve, their ship also left his dock but nobody actually saw the pilot entering the docking area!'

'Boy, wasn't Pete chatty,' said Morgana.

'Maybe it's 'cause he was so mad,' answered Faith.

'We already knew those holograms had left,' said Skye. 'One escaped with the green box; one was eliminated by Julius's acrobatics and the one with the red cap made a run for it.'

'What about their ship?' asked Julius.

'Maybe it was a hologram too,' said Skye.

'It can't have been. They saw it taking off from the dock,' answered Faith.

'Besides, if they do manage to kidnap this person, they're gonna need a real ship to transport him. Now we have two holos, a box and a ship missing,' recapped Morgana flatly. 'What are they gonna do – kamikaze themselves into the mess hall?'

'We can only keep our ears open,' said Julius with a sigh. 'But, between this latest news and the new Spring Mission rules, I bet Freja isn't sleeping all that well.'

'No one is,' added Faith seriously. 'Satras was packed with Zed officers. I've never seen so many since we got here.'

When they resumed their visits to the Hologram Palace, Julius saw that Faith had not exaggerated about the amount of Zed personnel patrolling the Lunar Perimeter. The Intra-Rail System was always crammed with men and women in uniform, sombre expressions on their faces. They would get off at Tijara, Tuala and Sield, at Satras and at the Docks, but the majority stopped at the Sea of Nectar, where the Curia was situated. The Hologram Palace was possibly the only place in Satras without officers present. The Mizki, it seemed, were still its main residents. The Skirts had picked up where they had left off with their winning streak and were still the leading team on the group charts. Often they simply played among themselves, other times they would sit in the courtyard, waiting for other students to challenge them or vice versa. It was a good way of meeting the Mizki from Tuala and Sield and, although they had decided to play only against groups from their year, they had been approached by older students as well, which really boosted their confidence. With the first proper flight simulation approaching, Julius had proposed that they lend a hand to any of their classmates who still weren't confident enough. Barth had been the first to gratefully accept their offer and, although the first few flights had gone horribly wrong, he had eventually

170

managed to hold his plane on course and to stop himself shooting team-mates by mistake.

On the first Friday of February, the 1MJ's made their way to level -5 of the holographic sector, where Professor Clavel was standing beside a closed door.

'Good morning Mizki. In the room behind me, you will find thirty Sim-Cougars waiting for you. Choose one, take your seat and strap yourself in. Don't touch anything else until I say so. On you go.'

Morgana was so excited that she pushed Faith and Skye unceremoniously out of the way.

'She's supposed to do that,' explained Julius, shaking his head.

They had never been in this particular room before, and Julius was really surprised by how large it was. Thirty aircrafts were lined up in rows of ten, all facing a raised podium at the foot of a huge white screen. Julius found an empty plane and stood there looking at it. The Cougar was metallic black with a transparent cover over the cockpit. He reckoned it was a good eight feet long, with a wing span of at least twenty feet. The wings bent backwards, like outstretched arms protecting the main body. It was shaped like a slim, elongated dewdrop, the tip of which was sharp and thin. The rounded back section hosted the engine.

Julius passed his hand over the slick surface of the Cougar, a smile breaking out on his face. There was a step ladder next to each plane and Julius used his to climb inside, being careful not to kick the plane. It was a tight fit but familiar nonetheless – the aircrafts in the Hologram Palace were modelled on the Cougars, and he had plenty experience with those. He pulled the seatbelt across his lap and waited. To his right, he saw Faith hovering over his plane and gently landing in his seat. When all the Mizki were ready, Professor Clavel climbed the steps to the podium. Julius saw that the teacher had a control panel in front of him and, as he pressed a button, all of the stepladders disappeared under the floor.

'You are sitting in the most advanced flight simulation program there is,' said Clavel. 'These Sim-Cougars are exact replicas of the real ones and, once we start, you will be able to manoeuvre them as you would if you were in space. For today you will not interact with each other, but instead concentrate on getting familiar and confident with your Cougars. This morning I want you to work on orientating around our lunar orbit, changing direction and controlling your speed, like we practiced in class. As you have learned in class, all Zed aircraft are capable of FTL, faster than light speed, no matter their size. Although you know how to engage FTL, it will be disabled for these simulations. The program will give you instructions as you progress through the various levels. Until you have satisfactorily mastered a task, you will not be allowed to progress further. Are you ready Mizki?'

'Yes, sir!' they all answered.

The hatch on Julius's plane closed down around him and locked into place.

'Good job I'm not claustrophobic,' he thought, taking a deep breath.

Slowly, four white walls emerged from the floor around his aircraft and rose all the way up to the ceiling. He guessed that he was now in a tank similar to those used for the Solo games in the Hologram Palace. The black body of his Cougar stood out sharply in all that white. Suddenly the light blinked out and Julius felt the plane lifting off the floor, the engine purring gently to life. A well lit runway appeared out of the darkness in front of him and the computer came on line.

'Prepare for launch,' said a voice from the console.

Julius followed the order and entered the launch sequence, as he had done in class so many times before.

'Engine engaged,' he said. 'Ready for departure.'

'Permission granted,' replied the computer flatly.

Julius pressed the thruster button and he was pushed against his seat by the G-force as the Cougar sprang forward towards the darkness at the end of the runway. As he entered the lunar orbit, his body relaxed again. He was aware that his surroundings were simulated, but the illusion was perfect. Decreasing his speed, he began to orient his plane toward the Moon. Zed, with all its buildings gathered under the shield, stood out clearly against its surface. He cheered loudly as a sense of joy overwhelmed him. Surely this was his coolest experience yet.

'Input Zed base coordinates from this position,' ordered the voice.

Julius complied. Now he could start his orientation training. The computer gave him the coordinates of different points in space to reach. Julius then had to find the correct spots, confirm their location and move onto the next one. He was curious to see how the others were doing, but all communications had been cut off. After about 20 correctly executed trips, he was allowed to return to base coordinates. With his Cougar still pointed at Tijara, he began to try some manoeuvres. Initially he had to practice using the thrusters to move his plane sideways, up and down. Julius was immediately aware that the controllers were set to a much higher sensitivity than those of the Cougars in the Hologram Palace. He continued to move his aircraft around until he felt confident. Then he was allowed to progress and practise turning at different angles.

'McCoy,' said Professor Clavel over the intercom.

'Yes, sir?' said Julius, a little startled.

'I want you to try a reverse 360 degree rotation from stationary, if you please.'

'Sir?'

'A back flip, McCoy! You do remember the sequence, I hope.'

'Yes, sir,' he answered, a small bead of sweat forming on his forehead.

In the Palace, he had never tried that manoeuvre before. He entered the command on the panel and gripped the control stick. The Cougar replied swiftly and Julius didn't even have time to realise he was upside down for a second or two before he was level again.

'Good,' said Clavel. 'Do a few more and then try a few forward flips.'

'Yes, sir.'

Full of confidence, Julius followed the instruction promptly. Next came the twists and those were a no-brainer for him. Finally, he was allowed to practise controlling the Cougar's speed. The aircraft was fast beyond imagination and even a simple acceleration made for an exhilarating experience. He spent the last hour combining all the different sections of that morning's training and after one final fast lap, ending in a back flip, a twist and a tight left turn, Julius made his way to the simulated hangar. As the program ended, he wasn't the only one to come out of the Cougar visibly excited. Morgana was jumping up and down while leaning on Faith, who was also bobbing out of control as a result.

'Miss Ruthier,' said Professor Clavel, suppressing a smile, 'I think

Mr Shanigan's suspensions may require a little more grace on your part.'

'I'm sorry, Professor, but this was the best lesson ever!' she said, beaming.

'And it won't be the last. This training is all you Mizki will be doing until your Spring Mission,' he said to the class. 'We are done for now. We shall resume at 14:00 hours. Dismissed.'

The excitement continued throughout their lunch. Julius and his mates didn't actually manage to eat much as they were too busy telling each other about their own performances. When the afternoon session resumed, they were all eager for more and Professor Clavel happily complied, programming the computer so that one scenario would follow the other without rest.

As the lessons continued throughout that February, they were eventually allowed to fly in teams. The Skirts were flying again, alternating the leadership of their squad every hour. The computer would set them scenarios – sometimes as simple as flying around moving obstacles, sometimes more complex like evading enemy ships, which were similar to the Cougars, only white. They couldn't use the catalysts yet, but they had plenty of other things to worry about as it was. When in charge, Julius had to check fuel levels and give instructions to his fighters to ensure that they would all survive the virtual attack. Evasive manoeuvres were becoming ever more important, and the simulator increased the difficulties of the scenarios with every tactical decision they made.

March brought an entirely new challenge for Julius and his classmates as Professor Clavel properly introduced them to the ship catalysts.

'About time,' whispered Skye, visibly thrilled.

For that lesson, Julius was flying by himself once again. As he waited in lunar orbit, Professor Clavel opened the intercom to all students.

'As you have probably noticed, there are two additions today. To your left and right, you will see the ship catalysts. They are the transparent levers protruding from the control panel. You will be using them to project your White skills. You cannot use the Mindkatas in this type of combat; therefore it is your Meditation training that you must rely on for focus and precision.'

'Glad I've got that sorted then,' said Julius, relieved.

'To fire, just do what you normally would. Aim the catalyst and focus your mind on the target. If you do this correctly, you will see your raw energy shooting out in a yellow beam. Now, for the real surprise of the day. As far as piloting is concerned, on a one-man vessel such as the Cougar, the controls change. When you are using the catalysts, you will be flying the ship using only your mind-skills.'

Shocked, Julius froze for a moment, as they had not been taught any such thing before.

'Before you panic, Mizki,' resumed Clavel, sounding slightly amused, 'the catalysts are very sensitive. They channel your energies through touch, but they also *feel* your will to move in whatever direction you want and take you there. Give it a try. Activate the combat program when you're ready.'

As soon as the intercom went silent, Julius started the firing simulation immediately. He was very eager to try out his skills on the catalysts.

'Proceed to the following coordinates to begin your training,' the computer intoned to him.

Julius quickly input them and flew towards a group of rocks. He chose a particularly large one and positioned his Cougar in a direct line opposite it. Closing his hands around the catalysts, he tightened his grip. As he touched the levers, a white circular target appeared on the glass in front of him. Instinctively, he thought that the Cougar needed to be a little over to the right. Immediately, he felt the ship shift to the right, exactly as he had wanted it to.

'This is just! It feels my thoughts,' he said, incredulous.

He adjusted the catalysts, until the crosshair glowed red and locked onto the rock. Julius focused his mind on it and pushed. He felt the familiar sensation of energy leaving his body and watched, open mouthed, as a bright yellow beam shot out from the tip of the Cougar and blasted the rock to smithereens.

'Who's the daddy!' he shouted excitedly.

He immediately moved on to the next rock, and the next, until they were all gone. The computer then challenged Julius to find and fire at enemy ships. As he engaged the different enemies, Julius was surprised to realise that he had been piloting the ship using only his mind, as his hands had never once let go of the catalysts. He spent the whole afternoon improving his single-fighter tactics and by the end of the lesson he had quite the sore head from concentrating and was a little on the weak side from using up so much energy.

These individual training sessions were entertaining enough but, after only a couple of them, Julius was itching to fly again with his mates. Professor Clavel, pleased with their progress, allowed them to try four-fighter squads. It was like being back in the Palace, only the Skirts were far more fluid now that they were using mind-skills to pilot and fight. Their confidence bordered on recklessness at times, which forced Clavel to hail them during training to remind them of where they were.

Whenever he reprimanded them, it was along the lines of, 'Skirts, get back into position and follow protocol. This is no game!' or 'Do I have to remind you of the difference between games and reality? If you die out there, it really is game over. Use your heads or I'll split your team up!'

That threat usually worked and they would all calm down again, until the next time. Except for the occasional *recommendations* from Clavel, Julius knew that he was making great progress in this subject. He was placing incredible demands on both his mind and body, but he knew it was worth it. Despite the tiredness, he never forgot to write home and tell Michael all about the Cougars, which made his brother really happy. He was careful not to mention anything about Salgoria's plans though, as he had the feeling that all correspondence would be monitored at a time like this. Although the Lunar Perimeter was not officially in a state of alert, Julius was aware of the increase in space traffic. At night, when he relaxed in the garden with the others, he could see dozens of Cougars flying over Zed every hour. By the end of March, their presence had become so much a part of the landscape that Julius hardly even noticed them as much anymore.

On top of this, two odd additions were introduced to their study programme. Professors Brown and Clavel gave a simulation lesson together, which involved learning to pilot and man a Stork, an eight-people carrier, on the routes from Zed to the regular colonies.

'This is very fishy,' said Morgana at the end of the lesson.

'What's fishy?' asked Julius.

'Well, Stork training and route lessons are not supposed to happen 'til third year. Kaori told me that she started them this past autumn. Why would they change the programme?'

'Maybe they want to make sure that even the MJ know enough to do their part if something happens,' suggested Skye.

Julius listened in silence. Skye's answer was as good as they were going to get and probably correct. What was bothering him, however, was something else. Ever since Faith had told them Pete's news, especially concerning the missing ship, Julius was unable to think about much else. When he lay in his bed at night, he would go over all the information in his head to try and make some sense out of it. In his mind he could clearly see the various pieces of the puzzle – the hologram remote control, the Scrambler, Red Cap, the missing ship, Kratos, even the flickering of Master Isshin – they were all linked somehow. He just couldn't see how. Sometimes he had the feeling that the answer was on the tip of his tongue but, before he could grasp it, it was gone.

In the second week of April, Professor King announced to the class that their Spring Mission would be carried out on Colonial 1, which instantly transformed Zolin Acalan, a 1MJ who happened to be from there, into an information kiosk. The poor boy was surrounded at all times of the day by classmates hoping to find out everything there was to know about the colony. A few days later, letters containing details of their mission were delivered to the students. Julius opened his at the dinner table and felt his stomach sink to his feet.

'Great,' he said gloomily.

'What's the matter? You look like a rain cloud,' said Faith worriedly.

'It says here that we leave on the 18th.'

'Hey, that's your birthday,' said Morgana, smiling.

'At 07:00 hours,' he continued grimly. 'An early rise – it's the present I've always wanted.'

'Cheer up, Julius,' grinned Skye, patting him on the back. 'We'll make it a birthday to remember!'

THE DRAW

Julius opened one blurry eye and poked his head out from under the cover. He could hear voices around him, but couldn't make the words out. Prising open his other eye, he was just in time to see Skye and Faith looming over his head. Faith was holding a blueberry muffin topped with a tiny lit candle.

'Happy birthday, sleeping beauty!' cried Faith happily.

'Make a wish,' said Skye.

Julius's brain took a few seconds to realise what was going on. He could feel in his bones that it was very-early-o'clock, but when they struck up an impressively deaf toned "Happy Birthday" in his honour, he couldn't restrain his smile.

'That was the nastiest birthday song I've ever heard. Thank you guys,' he said, sitting up in the bed.

'I thought we were doing quite well,' said Faith to Skye.

'Me too. Clearly he hasn't washed his ears yet.'

'That must surely be it,' said Julius.

'Here,' said Faith, passing the muffin to Julius. 'Make a wish and get dressed – it's already 06:30. We'll wait in the foyer.'

Julius looked at his candle. As the boys closed the door behind them, the flame flickered and went out.

'Hey, I haven't made a wish yet!' he said, disappointed. Given that he was going to wish for an extra hour in bed and knowing that was impossible, he shook his head and ate the muffin instead.

At 07:00 hours, Julius joined his classmates in Tijara's foyer. He had packed his rucksack the night before, just to gain some extra sleeping time, and he knew how to be quick when needed. Morgana gave him a big hug and wished him a happy birthday so loudly that all of the Mizki heard her. Faith didn't miss out on the opportunity for more singing.

'All together now,' he cried, hovering over the crowd, 'happy birthday to youuu ...'

Julius felt his cheeks burning and his ears melting. This chorus was even worse than Faith and Skye's earlier duet. Still, he managed a diplomatic smile and thanked everyone.

'If the celebrations are over, maybe we can begin the boarding procedure.' It was Captain Foster, wearing his usual "I'm not easily amused" expression.

The Mizki fell silent at once and bowed to Foster.

'In a moment, we shall make our way to the hangar,' said Foster. 'There are five Storks waiting there for you, piloted by our 5 Mizki Seniors. There will be a Zed officer to welcome you at Colonial 1. Remember, once you leave the Lunar Perimeter, you become a Zed representative. The reputation of us all depends on you. Be a gracious guest and a keen learner. Understood?'

'Yes, sir!' they answered in unison.

'Very well. Follow me,' said Foster, before opening the hangar gate and descending the stairs.

Julius shouldered his rucksack and followed his classmates. The access to Tijara's hangar was a brightly lit, white tunnel. Several corridors branched off to either side of them at regular intervals, but Julius couldn't see where they went to.

'A few signposts would have been good here,' said Faith, looking around curiously.

Morgana was visibly delighted to finally be able to see the school's hangar.

'I thought I heard an engine going, over there,' she said, as Julius dragged her back in line.

'It's a hangar, Morgana! What did you expect – your granny in a wheelbarrow?' he answered, pushing her forward.

'But it sounded *big.*'

Eventually the corridor opened onto a platform overlooking a shaft that was larger even than Satras. Julius walked to the rail, gaping in wonder, and looked down. He could see five different decks below him, each one lower than the previous one, opening outward like a giant fan. The first three of these decks had Cougars stationed on them; the last two were for the Storks. Dozens of Tijaran maintenance staff bustled to and fro, busy with upkeep and repairs for the planes. At the end of each deck, was a launch ramp built within a long tunnel and, from where he stood, Julius was able to witness a couple of breakneck Cougar re-entries, each one accompanied by Morgana's cheers and Faith's hollers.

'Let's move, Mizki,' called Foster, starting down a ladder that led off from the platform.

This time Julius literally had to prise Morgana's fingers away from the rail and drag her down the stairs, while Skye required the full weight of his body to push Faith along, much to the amusement of their classmates.

'Honestly, woman,' said Julius, shaking his head. 'You'll have your chance soon enough.'

'But they are sooo beautiful,' she sighed longingly.

When they reached the fourth deck, Foster motioned for them to board the Storks, and then walked all the way to the ship nearest the runway, where the 5MS pilots were waiting.

Julius and Skye, followed by Barth, boarded the last Stork left available, closest to the stairs. Faith and Morgana couldn't resist one last spot of sightseeing before boarding themselves. As they waited, Julius had a look around. The Stork was exactly the same as the one they had used during simulation. The two pilot chairs were at the front, with access to the various control panels. Behind them were the passenger seats, in two lines of four, facing each other. The access hatch was on the rear left hand side. There were two locked panels between the pilot and passenger seats on either side of the cabin, which Julius recognised as the access points for the ship's catalysts.

'You know,' said Morgana, stepping inside the Stork, 'we could have boarded one of the ships at the top.'

'Yes, we could've,' said Skye with a raised eyebrow, 'but we were too busy dragging you two gawping goons down here. Weren't we, Julius?'

'As a matter of –' Julius froze in mid sentence, his eyes fixed on the deck entrance.

'What's the matter?' asked Faith, hovering towards the hatch.

Julius had been watching two officers offloading crates at the mouth of a corridor leading off from the rear of the deck. Under the shadow of the stairs, he had not been able to see their faces, but as soon as they stepped into the light Julius's heart skipped a beat. As much as he wanted to be wrong, there could be no mistaking either of them – Master Isshin and Red Cap.

'Wait a minute ... isn't that Red Cap?' asked Faith, suddenly sounding very worried.

'Yes, together with my holopal,' said Julius.

'Why are they wearing Tijaran uniforms?'

'Whatever the reason, it can't be good.'

'What's going on?' whimpered Barth from his seat.

'Over there, at their feet,' said Morgana, looking out of one of the windows, 'it's the missing crate!'

Julius quickly spotted it, just as Red Cap looked up and took a step forward.

'Right on time,' he snarled, his eyes fixed on Julius. 'Try and catch me, White Child.'

Without hesitation, Julius leapt from the Stork, meaning to rush at him, when suddenly one of the crates exploded. He was hurled back inside the Stork, where he landed heavily on Skye. As he tried to regain his feet a second, much larger explosion shook the entire hangar. Julius managed to grab Morgana before she could crash into the hull plating.

'What's happening?' cried Barth, his whimpering replaced by sheer panic.

Julius gripped the edge of the door and leaned outside. There was debris everywhere and a number of small fires had broken out on the deck below. Several metres to the right, Captain Foster lay unconscious on the ground – Julius was relieved to see that two pilots were attending to him. A wailing siren filled the air and black smoke rose from those ships that had been damaged in the explosion. He could hear shouting all around him, as Tijaran security officers came pouring down the stairs.

'Attention!' a voice ordered from the hangar's loudspeaker. 'All Mizki return to Tijara assembly hall, immediately. All personnel to action stations.'

As the announcement was repeated again, Julius stepped onto the deck and continued searching for Red Cap and Isshin, but there was no trace of them.

'Barth, stop!' cried Morgana suddenly.

Julius turned and jumped out of the way just in time to avoid a full on collision with Barth, who was running towards the corridor entrance, where the missing crate had been left.

'Watch out!' shouted Skye, pointing to the walkway above Barth.

Julius looked up and saw a metal platform plunging towards the ground, directly where Barth was heading. He locked his eyes on Barth and gave him a mighty shove with his mind, sending him tumbling into the corridor as the platform crashed over the crate, blocking the entrance.

'Are you all right?' Julius shouted towards him.

Barth sat up and looked at him. He wore a dazed expression on his face and was breathing heavily.

'Yes, I... I think I tripped over this box,' he said, sounding confused.

Julius looked down and instinctively took a step back. The floor was littered with dozens of small red boxes, which he recognised as the holograms' remote controls. The moment Skye and Faith arrived by Julius's side, the red boxes started to vibrate madly, and in a matter of seconds they had all produced holographic humanoids in Tijaran uniforms.

'Barth, run!' cried Faith, gliding away from the crate and dragging Julius and Skye with him.

Barth didn't need to be asked twice and scampered down the corridor in a flash.

'Get back to the Stork!' yelled Julius.

As soon as the Arneshian holograms materialised, they started to scatter in all directions, mixing with the real Tijaran officers. Julius saw them boarding the Cougars and the few Storks left on the decks below them. As the ships took off some headed out into orbit, but a few of them deliberately crashed against the main hangar structure, hitting the stairs and blocking the corridors.

'We gotta get to the exit!' cried Skye, sheltering under a Stork wing.

'There's no time,' said Julius. 'The Stork is our only chance.'

He turned to Morgana and grabbed her shaking hands.

'Now's the time to show us what you've got. We need you to fly us out into orbit.'

Morgana looked at him, her eyes widened in panic. Gathering herself together, she took a deep breath and nodded.

'Get in boys. Faith,' she called to him, 'I'm gonna need your help.'

Faith followed her to the pilot seats.

'Skye, you and I will man the catalysts,' said Julius.

Skye closed the hatch and took his station. Julius unlocked his panel and pulled the catalyst towards him. As the radar screen lit up, he fastened the safety harness to keep himself steady.

'Hold on back there,' said Morgana, initiating the lift-off sequence. 'Faith, polarise the hull.'

The Stork vibrated slightly and hovered upward. Morgana was moving the ship forward when a Cougar cut them off, sending them veering downwards.

'Head for that runway below us!' cried Faith.

Morgana veered right and accelerated towards it. The Stork shot through the tunnel at such speed that the onboard computer self-activated.

'Reduce speed in hangar,' it said. 'You are breaking safety protocol 7.3.'

'Shut up!' cried Morgana, accelerating even more.

'Watch out for that rock! And for that one! And that one!' cried Faith, pointing in different directions all at once.

'Enough! Faith, you're supposed to calm me down here!' said Morgana, her voice almost hysterical.

'Sorry. You're doing just fine. You're the best pilot there is. You're great,' said Faith, sweating profusely.

'Get ready, guys,' she shouted over her shoulder as they sped towards the exit.

As the Stork entered orbit, Julius felt his lungs deflating slightly. Zed's space was riddled with ships – Tijara's, Tuala's and Sield's – all fighting against each other.

'This is a slaughter,' said Julius, as he watched a Cougar diving into the side of a Tuala Stork.

'I hope the others made it out in time,' whispered Morgana.

'The Zed shield has been hit!' cried Skye.

Julius looked on in dismay. The shield was flickering on and off as it absorbed stray hits from the fighting above it. He saw the individual shields of all Zed structures being activated for extra protection. Morgana flew the Stork higher, steering them out of harm's way.

'How can they drive?' said Faith, frustrated. 'They're not real.'

Julius looked at the battle raging below and suddenly it hit him. As the pieces of the puzzle fell into place, his face lit up.

'That's it!' he cried. 'They can't, but their remote controls can.'

'What are you talking about?' asked Morgana.

'Don't you see? Professor King said that, with powerful telekinetic skills, you can even pilot a spaceship from a distant location. The Arneshians don't have White Arts, so they're using VI technology instead!'

'That's impossible,' said Faith. 'You'd need some seriously powerful machines to remotely control those red boxes, and Arnesh is too far away for that.'

'But Kratos isn't. That's why they've occupied it!'

Julius looked at his friends as the reality of his words dawned on them.

'I'm going there,' he said steadily. 'Anyone wants to pull out, now's the time.'

'I'm in,' said Skye flatly, holding Julius's gaze.

'My sister is down there,' said Morgana. 'There's no way I'm not coming. Faith?'

'All the way, Skirts.'

Julius felt a weight lifting from his heart. 'Morgana, set a course for Kratos. Faith, send a transmission to Cress. Tell him to scan the fleet. The ships without any bio signatures are piloted by holograms. Skye and I will be on defence.'

Skye nodded and moved back to his station. Morgana entered the coordinates for Kratos into the computer and they slipped out of Zed orbit undetected.

'Done,' said Faith, pressing a button. 'I've sent the message. Let's hope he gets it.'

A minute later, Cress's voice echoed in the ship. 'Stork 9, this is Tijara. We've received your message. Re-enter Zed orbit immediately. I'm sending the coordinates for a safe rendezvous.'

Faith shook his head as he began to jam the transmission. 'Tijara, this is Stork 9. We're having trouble reading you. Repeat.'

Cress's voice started to crackle. 'Stork 9 ... ordered ... immediately ...'

'Sorry sir, I can't hear you,' Faith said.

Finally the line went dead.

'I can't believe I just did that,' he said, looking nervously at the others. 'They'll take away me skirt and give me leaded bloomers for this.'

That thought made them laugh so much that Morgana had to activate the autopilot.

'Yeah, yeah. Laugh it up,' said Faith, but he couldn't hold back a smile either.

'How long till we get there, Morgana?' asked Julius once the laughter had subsided.

'Well, according to the computer, Kratos is 0.01953125 light years away.'

'In English please?' asked Skye.

'Och, a hyperjump will get us there in a tick. Why?'

'Because, if I'm reading this radar right, we've got company,' said Julius.

'I see it,' said Faith, checking the scan readings, 'but I don't recognise the ship.'

'Friendly?' asked Morgana nervously.

'No bio signatures onboard. It's a nasty.'

Julius looked through the rear hatch window. The ship was as large as the Zed shuttle that had taken them to the Moon. It was speeding towards them but, instead of opening fire, a ramp opened outward and downward, like a giant mouth.

'Why isn't it engaging us?' asked Morgana, keeping the Stork clear of it.

'Because it can't,' answered Julius. 'You can't use the catalyst without mind–skills. Besides, that doesn't even look like a Zed vessel.'

'It's trying to scoop us up,' said Morgana.

'Ahead!' cried Faith. 'It's an asteroid field. Let's lose it in there before we make the jump. I don't fancy playing cat-and-mouse in hyperspace.'

'Put some air between us, Morgana,' yelled Skye. 'Give us a chance at a clear shot.'

The Stork accelerated and entered the field from below. The rocks were hurtling past them, some of them spinning erratically. Julius could see droplets of sweat forming on Morgana's brow.

'Just like in the games, Morgana,' encouraged Skye. 'We know you can do it.'

Julius saw the vessel approaching on their right, with only a large asteroid between them.

'Morgana, get ready to slow down at my command!' he cried. 'Skye, it's gonna come out in front of us.'

Julius followed the ship on his radar and saw it converging toward their trajectory. He held tight to the catalyst and adjusted his grip.

'Three ... two ... one ... now!'

The Stork suddenly decelerated, just in time to avoid crashing into the enemy, which had popped out just in front of them. Julius concentrated on his target. Even though he was sure the pilot wasn't Red Cap, it was his face that he imagined. He pushed hard with his mind and felt the familiar sensation of energy coursing from his body and into the catalyst. At the same time, two yellow beams – his and Skye's – shot out of the Stork and struck the ship directly on its engine. The explosion rocked the Stork, shaking it off course, but it was nothing that Morgana couldn't handle.

'Come to mama!' shouted Skye, giving Julius a high-five.

'The Skirts are back,' laughed Faith, patting Morgana on the shoulder. 'Nice bit of flying, girly-o.'

She relaxed, looking exhilarated. 'It's time to jump, guys. Just hold on to something.'

'Wait a minute,' Faith stammered nervously, 'are you sure you know how to do this? I mean, we've never actually done it bef ...'

Morgana didn't allow him to finish his argument and fired up the hyperdrive.

Julius was overwhelmed by a strange sensation of displacement, like he had temporarily stepped outside of his body. Fortunately, it lasted no more than a couple of seconds before the feeling subsided and a giant metallic disc appeared in front of them.

'Looks like Kratos's shield is still operational,' said Faith, pointing at the shimmering layer that cupped the disc. 'I'm going to scan the surface.'

'Check for bio signs too,' said Julius. 'The Arneshians may be there.'

'No humanoid presence. In fact, no life forms whatsoever,' said Faith, after a short pause. 'The only thing I'm picking up is a small cubic structure. It must be the holocontrol station we're looking for.'

'I'll take us right above it,' said Morgana.

The Stork approached the Arneshian outpost and brought them through the shield unscathed. Morgana steadied the ship and landed it next to their target.

'It doesn't look like much,' said Morgana. 'Is the computer inside?'

'Kids,' said Faith seriously, 'we have a problem. According to our scanner, that cube *is* the main computer. And we can't blow it up. It's made of some sort of extra-strong inorganic alloy.'

'What if all four of us link to the catalysts?' asked Skye.

'That could work ... if you were able to go nuclear.'

'Then we disable the mainframe manually.'

'Not possible. It's right in the core,' answered Faith, pointing at the schematics on his screen.

'So what, we just go back?' cried Skye, frustrated.

'No we don't,' said Julius calmly. 'There is another way.'

From the moment Faith had mentioned the word "inorganic", Julius's mind had instinctively zoomed in on his draw ability, and the day he had stopped Professor Turner's watch. It was a long shot, and a dangerous one at that, but he couldn't think of any other way. Marcus Tijara himself had proven that it was possible.

'I think I can draw from it,' continued Julius.

'From a non-living source? You're kidding, right?' said Faith.

'No I'm not. But you better be ready to fly us out on the double 'cause I don't know how long I can hold on to that energy for.'

'Forget it, mate. It's too risky. It could kill you,' said Faith seriously.

'I've done it before, Faith. I can release the cube's energy through the catalyst. It's the only chance we've got and we're wasting time. You have to trust me on this one.'

They stared at him in silence and he saw dark wisps rising from their heads. Julius looked away and opened the hatch. They were scared and he couldn't risk getting his mind muddled up with fear as well. He needed all the focus he could muster.

'Just be ready,' he said.

Julius climbed out of the Stork and walked over to the computer. As he moved towards it, the black exterior of the cube shimmered in the artificial sunlight from its shield. Julius stopped in front of it and watched as algorithms and dim flickering lights passed over its shiny

192

surface. He walked around the cube a few times, hoping to find a focal point, and eventually stopped at its east side. Here was a darker area, which the scrolling information was streaming into, almost as if it was an entrance to the inner core itself. There was no way to be absolutely sure, but he had to make a decision.

Vigorously, he rubbed his hands together, trying to get the blood flowing through his fingertips, and placed them near the surface. His fingertips did not touch it, but he could still feel his skin tingling all over from being so close to the cube's energy field. He closed his mind to everything else around him, to the noises, the light and the faces of his mates. He let the air out of his lungs gently and, when there was no more to push out, he took a deep, steady breath and held it in. His mind was immediately filled with images of a blue, smoky fluid, moving up through his fingers and arms like a snake. The sensation was far more overpowering than that first draw in class had ever been. The fluid moved into his chest where it gathered in his lungs. When his whole body felt like it was on fire, Julius knew he had to stop.

Forcing his eyes open, he released the air from his lungs. His legs were shaking so much that Julius fell to his knees, breathing heavily. He felt sick, as if he had just drunk some sort of poison but, when he looked at the cube again, a pained grin touched his lips. The computer had gone almost totally dark, with only a handful of lights still visible. Julius forced himself back to his feet and staggered in the direction of the Stork.

Skye had jumped out of the ship, and had his arms outstretched, reaching for him. 'Let me help you.'

'Don't touch me!' said Julius, recoiling from him.

Skye looked down at Julius's hands – the palms were raw-red and wet.

'OK. I won't touch you, but I'll help you along.'

Julius felt his body being lifted from the ground and pushed smoothly towards the Stork and knew that it was Skye's doing. Then Faith appeared at the hatch and locked his eyes on Julius too. He floated right inside the Stork and landed gently in front of one of the catalysts. He glanced at Morgana, who looked like she had just stopped crying, and managed a tired smile in her direction.

'Let's go, pilots,' said Skye, closing the door.

The Stork took off immediately and shot away from the cube, sending ripples through the shield's membrane. Julius knew that, if he held onto the computer's energy for even one more minute, he would explode. Grabbing the catalyst, he focused on the target and discharged all the energy in one mighty push. A thick yellow beam shot out of the Stork, disintegrating the cube in a massive explosion. The Stork was propelled forward by the blast and it was only thanks to Skye's quick reflexes that Julius wasn't thrown around like a ragdoll. Kratos's disc had snapped in two and the pieces were slowly drifting off into space.

'You did it!' shouted Morgana. She jumped from her seat and swung her arms around Julius. 'Your mum will never forgive me,' she said, half crying and half laughing. 'I promised her I'd keep you out of trouble!'

'That was amazing,' said Skye. 'If you make it back alive, they'll put you in a museum.'

Julius couldn't help but smile, even though he was still dazed and his hands were in agony. Thankfully, Morgana had found a first aid kit and was carefully bandaging them.

'Hey guys,' called Faith from the front of the Stork, 'the cavalry has just arrived, and they're all human.'

A fleet of Cougars had just entered Kratos's airspace and was closing in on the Stork.

'Open a channel, Faith,' said Skye, moving toward the cockpit.

'Tijara, this is Stork 9,' announced Faith confidently. 'The enemy is down. Mission accomplished, and thank you very much. Oh, we also got rid of that useless disc for you, by the way.'

Julius and the others looked at him, shaking their heads in a mixture of disbelief and amusement.

Faith turned to face them, sporting his characteristic grin. 'I'll be deported to the Halls of Ahriman for that but, heck, it was worth it!'

'I told you we'd give you a birthday to remember, McCoy,' said Skye, sitting down next to Julius.

'Yeah,' said Julius wearily. 'But please, let's make it a bit less memorable next year.'

BELONGING

Julius dozed in and out of sleep during the brief journey back. His head was throbbing and his muscles were sore and stiff. Everyone was quiet, but he knew their silence was deceptive. They were all aware of the importance of what they had just done on Kratos and the number of people they had potentially saved, but they weren't going to brag about it. Somehow, it didn't feel like the right thing to do.

As their ship entered the lunar orbit, Julius could see debris floating everywhere – the remains of the defeated Cougars. Dozens of Sky-Jets zoomed in and out of Pete's docking base, salvaging what they could. Morgana landed the Stork in Tijara's hangar, which was being repaired at an impressive speed. Captain Foster was waiting for them on the runway. His head was bandaged, but he looked his usual stern self.

'Come with me, Mizki,' he said, bowing slightly to them.

They followed him in silence back to Tijara, all the way to the hall outside Cress's office, where he left them without a word.

'Humph. He could've at least said something nice,' said Faith once Foster had left.

'Did you expect a brass band?' answered Skye, dropping heavily onto a seat.

'No, but a "Thank you for saving our lives" type of thing would have been good.'

'It'll be a miracle if they don't court martial us.'

Morgana had just helped Julius to sit down, when suddenly the office door opened, making them all jump up in surprise.

'Inside,' said Cress curtly.

They filed into the office and waited quietly before the Grand Master. Cress walked behind his desk and stood by Freja's side. They both looked extremely serious.

'Miss Ruthier,' said Cress, 'I want a full account of your actions, from the moment you entered Tijara's hangar. Don't leave anything out, not even Mr Shanigan's amazing ability for jamming fleet channels.'

Julius saw a red wisp shooting out of Faith's head, but managed to keep a straight face. As Morgana recounted the day's events, Julius became increasingly aware of Freja's gaze on him. When she reached the part in which he had drawn from the computer, he saw Freja's eyes widen, just for a second. When Morgana finished her account, nobody spoke for a short while. Freja and Cress studied the desk panel. Julius watched Freja touching various areas of the screen, sorting through data and grouping information into folders. Finally, he looked at Cress and nodded.

'I thought we'd already discussed the Zed protocol of acting as a collective,' said Cress.

'Permission to speak freely, sir,' said Julius, trying his best to not sound rude.

'Granted,' answered Cress.

'I am aware that we are only 1MJ, sir, but we understand teamwork.' As he said that, he looked quickly at his friends, who all nodded encouragingly. 'The thing with being a Zed officer is that life is not so much about choice, but more about duty. We had the choice of turning back the Stork and watching the slaughter of our fellow Mizki, but we had the duty, the knowledge and the opportunity to put a stop to it. So we did. And for that we take full responsibility.'

The room fell silent for a few seconds.

Finally, the Grand Master spoke: 'The list of infractions committed today is more than enough to have you expelled.'

Julius felt Skye shifting uncomfortably next to him.

'However,' continued Freja, visibly relaxing, 'we also need to recognise the importance of individual initiative, especially when that initiative is undertaken for the greater good of our family. You have all displayed incredible skills today. Miss Ruthier's evasive manoeuvres would have matched those of an experienced pilot.'

Morgana blushed instantly and stared at her feet.

'Mr Shanigan's co-piloting and Mr Miller's use of the catalyst in combat were also of the highest standard.'

Faith and Skye allowed themselves a shy grin.

'And, of course, Mr McCoy's leadership skills, and the clever use of the rare gift that is inorganic drawing, were just exceptional.'

Julius bowed his head, a flush of pride awoken in him by those words.

'Foiling Salgoria's plot was a remarkable achievement, Mizki. No charges will be pressed against any of you. All I will say is that you must learn to trust in your family from now on. It is unity that makes us stronger. And now, follow Master Cress to the infirmary. Mr McCoy, please stay a little longer. Dismissed.'

Apprehensively, Julius watched his friends leave. He had never been alone with the Grand Master and he hoped Freja wasn't going to give him some kind of special punishment, given that he had already singled him out as the "leader".

'As your Stork was re-entering Tijara, Mr List came looking for me quite urgently,' said Freja, opening a drawer.

Julius watched as he placed a box on the desk and, when he opened it, Julius's heart sank. There was a red cap inside it.

'I believe this was left for you,' said Freja, handing it to him.

Julius took it and noticed a piece of paper pinned to the inside lining. It read "I'll get you McCoy. You can't run forever, White Child."

'Where did they find it, sir?' asked Julius, stunned, the happiness of a moment ago completely gone.

'Apparently Master Isshin's VI program activated itself in the presence of Mr List. It lasted only a few seconds but, as it vanished, it left behind one of the red control boxes and this. I remembered your previous encounter with the hologram you called "Red Cap" in the hangar and, of course, he played a rather big part in today's events according to Miss Ruthier's account. Am I correct to assume that it taunted you?'

Julius nodded, his mouth too dry to say anything.

'Don't let it get to you. Never let emotions cloud your harmony. If you are meant to meet it again, you will. But remember, this hologram, as intelligent as it seems, is still just a program, not real. Salgoria, on the other hand, is our main concern. Have a seat, Mr McCoy.'

Julius was grateful for the offer, as he was feeling rather light headed.

'Do you know what a White Child is?' asked Freja, easing the chair in behind the desk.

'No, sir. But ... Red Cap called me that this morning, inside the hangar.'

Freja nodded. 'I shall tell you what we know on this topic, since it concerns you personally. It is no secret that the Arneshians have tried to gain power over humanity since Zed was created. Over the centuries, their rulers devised different plans to achieve their objective but, fortunately for us and thanks to Zed, they were never successful. When Salgoria became queen, she changed her tactics. No longer would control be gained by useless open war, but by using the very abilities that made the Arneshians so gifted in the first place – the Grey Arts, or advanced technological and logical skills. The holographic remote control is just one example of the devices they can invent. When it comes to new technology, they are still unbeatable.

'In recent years, however, Salgoria has also begun meddling with genetic engineering – manipulating the DNA of an organism. Tell me, McCoy, have you heard of Bastiaan Grant?'

'Yes, sir. I was told he was one of the people who got kidnapped and that he died, possibly because of some sort of medical experiment.'

'Precisely. The people abducted were all Zed members, with very advanced mind-skills. I was one of the crew members who found Angra Mainyu, the Arneshian lab where Mr Grant was experimented upon. We also discovered the bodies of those who disappeared before him. Most shocking was the discovery of many lifeless infants. The notes left behind by their medical team confirmed what we had already started to realise: Salgoria was trying to craft the perfect being. This perfect DNA would be genetically created through the unwilling donations of people like Grant and the Arneshians themselves. Remember, she needs an Arneshian because only one of them can fully reach the maximum potential of the Grey Arts.

'However, things did not go according to plan. The experiments failed and Salgoria decided that, in order to succeed, she would need someone as gifted as Tijara himself had been, someone who would possess the most powerful White and Grey Arts and would be called by Tijara's own nickname – a White Child.'

Julius was staring at Freja, dumbstruck. 'Sir,' he said, 'you cannot possibly mean that I am one of those. There must be a mistake. I mean, I even had to take remedial meditation!'

'Your Brain Augmentation chart, Red Cap's actions, and the way you foiled Salgoria's plans beg to differ, Mr McCoy. It is also apparent to me that the ship that pursued you was clearly there to kidnap you. Don't forget, you're only thirteen and have a lot of training ahead of you to fully unlock your potential. Salgoria will not try such direct tactics again in a hurry, not now that she knows what you're capable of. But be on your toes, for people like you are always on her radar.'

Freja stood up and Julius respectfully did likewise.

'I didn't mean for us to have this conversation so soon, or to make you aware of your potential in such a fashion, but circumstances forced my hand. Perhaps it is for the best. Off you go now. I believe Dr Walliser will want to run some tests on you. The draw you performed today will fill up several library chips.'

'Thank you, sir,' said Julius, bowing his head.

As he opened the door, he glanced at the Grand Master one last time. Freja's grey eyes looked back and Julius was filled with that same sense of admiration that he had felt upon first seeing his portrait back on Earth. He was indeed very proud to belong to the Tijaran family.

By the end of April, news of the attack on Kratos had made its way around all of Zed, and the Skirts had become well known, even outside the gaming circle. Julius had told only Morgana about his conversation with Freja. Somehow, he was embarrassed to admit to the guys that he had been at the centre of the Queen of Arnesh's plans and that she had singled him out as a White Child. He most definitely wasn't going to tell his parents about it either – he was sure they would rush to fetch him, out of fear for his life. He would be careful, as Freja had said, and that was all he could do. There was no way he would let anybody, even an evil queen, ruin his dream of becoming a Zed officer.

Although Julius and his friends had decided to keep it quiet, or "play it cool" as Skye had put it, Barth had not been able to refrain from telling his classmates about how Julius had saved him in the hangar. Naturally, none of the Mizki could rest until they knew more, and so they had badgered and pestered the Skirts, until the whole story had come out and was then spread to the entire school. Kaori, who was understandably very proud of her little sister, had seen to it that Tuala also knew all about it, and it was only a matter of time before the Sield students were in the loop too.

By mid-May, it had become impossible for Julius to go anywhere without being cornered and questioned about their fight, and especially about his draw. He wasn't really the public speaker type and, although he was proud of their achievement, he really wished they would just give it a rest and let him get on with things. When Dr Walliser released the first part of his research on Julius's draw to Tijara's library, an incredible amount of students and workers from the Curia flocked there to read it. Fortunately, this release gave Julius a welcome break from being interrogated at every possible opportunity. In fact, the students seemed to be so in awe of him that they appeared hesitant to approach him anymore, which suited Julius perfectly.

On the 31st of May, the spring term ended and the Mizki were all packed and ready for departure to their summer camps. Faith would spend his three months at Pit-Stop Pete, learning about the everyday running of a docking station and the various maintenance routines of the fleet. Morgana was going with him for two months before joining, under special permission, the apprentice flying camp in the Canis Major constellation. Julius, with the personal approval of Master Cress, had decided to go to the Fornax constellation, where Zed held intensive training courses on the different uses for ship catalysts. He was really looking forward to it for two reasons: on the one hand he would be travelling 46 light years away from Earth, his very first interstellar journey and the fulfilment of a childhood dream; on the other he would have a chance to fully test his mind-skills. As an added bonus, he wasn't going alone, as Skye had decided to join him.

Julius and his classmates walked to the Zed dock, where they would soon board the transports to their various destinations. Julius watched the students saying their goodbyes to each other. There were plenty of pats on the back for the boys and emotional hugs between the girls. To Julius it looked just about right: out here they were all family after all.

'It seems like yesterday that I first landed on the Moon,' said Morgana, reminiscing.

'Actually, that was Neil Armstrong,' said Faith with a grin.

Morgana looked at him in mock exasperation.

'She's right,' said Skye, 'and what a great year it's been.'

'Hear, hear,' cried Faith.

'And you know what made it so good?' said Julius, beaming. 'The Skirts did. And it's only the beginning.'

Lightning Source UK Ltd.
Milton Keynes UK
UKOW020601290911

179446UK00002B/8/P